JILL WAGNER

THE MOTHER KILLER SERIES

BOOK 1

Jane's JOURNEY

Jane's Journey

Book design by www.delaney-designs.com

Acknowledgment

Thank you for choosing my breakout novel, Jane's Journey.

So many people deserve to be recognized for their help and support during my journey through this process. It's hard to admit, being a writer and all, that it's hard to find words strong enough to express how grateful I am to so many people. For my friends, and my husband, Al, who supported me and understood my 'absence' while I worked. Deb and Vicky, your faith in me and your encouragement boosted me more than you'll ever know.

To my youngest (baby girl) daughter, Kelly, in spite of your crazy busy life, you always had my back and offered your support and I appreciate you.

For my bonus daughter, Kristy, I will always be grateful for your positive feedback. It meant the world to me and helped me forge ahead even when I didn't think I could, or even should.

And most especially for my daughter, Shay. Even just the looks you gave me when I shared my doubts and frustration helped keep me going. I can't even put into words how much your belief and encouragement meant to me. And of course, if not for your expertise at all things social media, not to mention your amazing marketing ideas, and book cover design, my path to this point would've been 'fraught with peril'. I appreciate all your help more than you know.

Thank you everyone – I love you all.

PROLOGUE

IONIA STATE PENITENTIARY – IONIA, MICHIGAN

4-10-2010 – Six months ago

My name is Tad Wilkins, but to the penal system that has provided me with three squares and a bunk for 13 years, I'm known only as Inmate 67049. I find it ironic that a system designed to rehabilitate would erase the name of a man who has seen and done things that make most nightmares seem like fairy tales.

I am that man and will never be rehabilitated because I was born with a stillborn soul. They can provide all the computer classes, library books and therapy in the world and it isn't going to change who I am. The professionals that call themselves experts have diagnosed me as being a psychopath and a narcissist. I've been researching this since I was 10 years old and they're probably accurate. The fact that the only thing I love is hearing a woman first plead for her life, and then as the will is tortured out of her, beg for death is a damn good indicator that my mind works differently than a neurotypical brain. What my highly intelligent mind can't understand is why everyone doesn't think like me. For me, watching the lights go out in a woman's eyes is my reward for a job well done. I am the best there ever was, and now it's time for me to take on a protégé. I will not allow my legacy to be forgotten...ever.

I've been inside for 13 years and have spent that time growing a network of underground associates because I knew my days of exerting power and control were not over. And while governing the people inside of my insulated world was a nice challenge, it was not as fulfilling as commanding when a life would end, and I had to be ready to take my skills to the next level. When the FBI finally caught up to me, they had enough to charge me with 15 kills in seven years. I actually started practicing several years earlier, killing prostitutes from the inner city, but try as they might, the bureau could not connect me to them. However, being the smartest man in the game did not serve me with my plan to mold my daughter, Jane, into a killing partner. Those plans were destroyed on the day they broke down my door and arrested me in front of her. I was outraged that I never had a chance to provide her with the proper training, but with her career path forged, the time is now for me to groom my successor.

I haven't been a killer my whole life; in fact I worked hard at hiding what the masses would call my abnormal psychopathy for many years. I earned six figures as an architect, lived in a middle-class subdivision in Holly, Michigan, and was the widower that all the housewives wanted to take care of. My wife died of brain cancer when Jane was only two months old. All the years I'd spent developing my charismatic, easy-going persona finally paid off. The role of grieving father was the perfect cover for me to begin fulfilling my true calling.

When I was 10 and trying to figure out why the other 5th graders called me a mean bully, I found myself with the school's social worker a lot. I sensed she would not like my honest answers to the questions she asked about how I felt when I made my classmate cry, or if I was mad at Sally when I poked her in the eye with a pencil and how it made me feel. It was then that I realized I was special and didn't think like others. So, being the smartest person in the room, I instinctively knew not to tell her that I felt nothing except exhilarated when the pencil tip became buried in her spongy ocular fluid.

The social worker and school counselors told my mother that I was too young to clinically diagnose as a narcissist or a psychopath, but I was more than likely headed in that direction.

They recommended therapy which I vehemently refused, but the experience did teach me how to hide. I learned that getting the best grades (which was easy for me), and being the sweetest and best-groomed young man in the community got me far more of the accolades I craved, than being the mean, creepy kid in the back row. What I didn't realize at 10 years old, was that the facade I was so painstakingly perfecting, would become monotonous to the point of exhaustion.

After I earned a full ride scholarship to Michigan State University, I happily faced, and of course successfully mastered, an adult level of pretentious deception. I was such a master of disguises, that the firm I chose, and the woman I decided to marry, actually believed they'd sought *me* out. Hannah was the woman I made my wife. She was the perfect adornment for my arm at business functions, because she was as smart as she was beautiful, and knew exactly how to take care of me. I worked hard on this new deceptive cloak, which was easy to maintain and refine, as long as I was able to keep my wife away from her sister, Judy. She was a renowned psychologist and on the few times I had to be with her, I felt like her eyes were boring deep into mine, looking for a soul that didn't exist. Judy lived 700 miles away, in Richmond, Virginia, so if she happened to visit, I'd simply have a business trip out of town.

My wife became pregnant shortly after we were married, and I was excited about it because I needed a new challenge, and knew I'd have to adjust the veil I'd gotten so good at living behind. When she refused lifesaving treatment for the tumor on her brain in order to preserve the life of her unborn child, I was enraged. The world I'd so shrewdly built over the years was at risk, and I knew that if I wanted to keep the air of perfection from crumbling, I needed an outlet for the socially unacceptable proclivities I'd kept at bay since I poked Sally in the eye with a pencil.

I started killing with the high-risk, low-profile females that worked the urban streets of Pontiac at night. I had no specific type.

I acted purely on instinct and timing, and I had never felt so liberated and free in my life. It all came down to the power. All my life I'd been exercising a sort of power over people's perceptions, but the power over life and death was my ultimate calling, and I craved it. I had nothing personal against any of the women I killed, but when I beat and tortured them until they begged for death, and then squeezed their last breaths from their lungs, I felt alive. When I would come home to the nurse or concerned neighbor I had hired to care for the newborn child, I found it much easier to pull the veil back in place and be the grieving father everyone expected me to be.

Even though I was a new and inexperienced killer, I was smart enough to leave no traces of myself behind, and to spread my kills around multiple cities. There was no pattern to my rampage, so neither the FBI, nor the State of Michigan ever connected them to me. Yet with no one knowing I was out there, my kills became just a temporary outlet, like a flash-bang moment of euphoria that fizzled out to barely a spark. I needed to find another way to keep the fizzle bright and burning between kills.

It is true that most serial killers hone their skills and take the 'leave nothing behind' approach to evade capture, but most of us want someone to know we're out there. We thrive on our power to create fear and terror on society. Hell, it's what drives us. Once I focused in on young mothers, and developed my own methodology, following my kills on the news was like an aphrodisiac and kept me satisfied while I chose my next target. I chose the women I wanted very carefully, and then spent six months getting to know their habits and routines. Women, especially those with babies, seem to function on a predictable timetable. They're also fighters, which any killer will tell you, enhances the experience.

For seven years I was able to be the doting father everyone expected while still fulfilling my need to hunt, abduct and kill. I took only two women a year during that time but found that the hunt was almost as thrilling as the actual kill. There is a lot of power in knowing that you are in control of someone's life, and death, even before you have them writhing in zip-ties.

In a way only a narcissistic psychopath can understand, on the day the FBI finally caught up with me, I felt almost relieved. I could finally drop the array of masks I'd worn for so many years, and just be myself. Once I was incarcerated I found that having no mask, and no filter, served me well. Being perceived as bat shit crazy went a long way toward gaining alliances and favors. It was my outside affiliations that helped me keep track of Jane, and since I'd been robbed of the joy in making her a killer, I figured it was my right to sabotage her life as an adult.

I knew she was a rising star at the FBI training academy at Quantico. What she didn't know, however, was that she was going to become one of the puppets on my string in the making of The New Mother Killer. I already had my protégé chosen, and it was only a matter of time before he was clamoring to learn my secrets, and then, all I'd have to do is control the strings.

CHAPTER ONE

DAY ONE - REAGAN INTERNATIONAL AIRPORT - ARLINGTON VA

October 19, 2010 – 5:00AM

Traffic on I-95 heading into Reagan International Airport was usually gridlocked with commuters who generally fell into one of three categories: the first group would engage in a symphony of horns, while the second spent their traffic time on cellphones, either barking orders or setting meetings, and the third group were the ones who, knowing the delays they'd face, left home with a giant coffee, plenty of time and a book on tape.

Traffic was not an issue at 5:00 am, as FBI Agent trainee, Jane Newell, stared through the misty fog at the lights that flickered on the airport's tower. She could almost feel the almond-colored eyes of her best friend, training agent, and mentor boring into her. Jane appreciated that Kate was giving her time to process the fact that they were racing to the airport to meet with a team of agents and were headed to the town where her childhood came to an abrupt halt. Holly, Michigan, is where she lived when her father, Tad Wilkins, was arrested for serial murder. Not only was she going back there for the first time in 13 years, but their case was to find Tad's copycat murderer.

Jane was aware of the protocol that should have disqualified her from the task force, and knew that Kate, and Unit Chief, Bill, had to have made a compelling case with the director, or she wouldn't be here, and she wanted to be a part of this team more than anything because it would be a great step toward atonement for the vile actions of her father.

Kate's screeching stop, and the jerking of the SUV when she rammed it into park, brought Jane from her thoughts as they grabbed their bags and got out of the car.

"Hustle up, girl," Kate barked, "the team is waiting on us." With legs that practically reached her arm pits, Jane was able to match Kate's jogging pace with just a fast walk. Kate stopped short as they approached the aircraft's stairs and turned to Jane.

"Pay attention to my words," she said, "you're out of time here, so shake the cobwebs from your brain, and start acting like an agent. If you have any concerns about working this case, well, stow them because that's the job. Bill and I went to the mat to get you added to this task force, so don't blow the opportunity to kick some ass and prove to them that you've got what it takes to put your personal feelings away and be an amazing agent. You can put those feelings away, can't you?"

Jane nodded, and was grateful for her mentor's straight forward, no nonsense approach because it always grounded her in a clear reality. As they climbed the steps, Jane reminded herself that she was not a 15-year-old girl anymore, that her father was powerless over her, and that these were not his victims. Before the plane door opened, she looked straight at Kate and stated, "I worked my ass off to get here. I will not blow it. You have my word."

After their bags were stowed, Kate went to the front of the plane for coffee and Jane took a seat across from her boss; just like Kate, Bill had a way of getting right down to business.

"Welcome to the task force, Jane. I'll make the introductions once we're in the air. Abbey, our analyst will also be joining us from Quantico with more details."

Jane nodded but didn't speak because she sensed there was more to come. "Jane, I agreed with Kate, and plead the case to the director to get you on this task force because I hoped that you'd be able to bring a unique perspective to it, but I need to know that you're going to be able to handle it. I know you pushed yourself harder than any of the other recruits at the academy, and I'd like to know why. I won't have a rogue agent and want to be assured that this case won't trigger memories you may not be able to handle."

Jane trained her whiskey brown eyes on Bill, and since she'd spent countless hours reliving and then filing away her darkest memories, was quick with her reply.

"My memories don't need a trigger, sir, because they're always there. I can handle them, and as far as why I worked so hard at the academy, I have two answers. First and most important is to make amends, and secondly, I know Kate pulled some strings to get me in and I did not want to disappoint her. Besides, she would have kicked my ass."

Bill smiled at the levity she added, and then asked what she meant by amends.

"I want to make amends to the families my father ruined, by putting monsters just like him in cages for the rest of their lives."

Bill seemed happy with her response, and added, "I told the team that Wilkins is your father. Our best hope at solving this quickly is if everyone has as much information as possible, and quite honestly, I wanted eyes on you. You have the promise of being a great agent, but not if we burn you out on this first case." Jane acknowledged that she understood as Kate sat down beside her and the captain announced they'd been cleared for departure.

Once the seat belt light went off, Bill stood up to formally introduce the task force.

"We have two new agents with us today. On my right is Jane Newell, a recent graduate from Quantico. Her academy performance was among the best I've seen, and I think we will benefit from her input."

Jane was slightly uncomfortable at all the accolades but smiled at the new faces as Bill went on. "Our other new agent is a veteran with the bureau, Adrian Sanchez, and is on loan to us from the cyber unit. I'm sure his expertise will be an asset. The gentleman with more salt than pepper in his beard sitting beside him, is Seth Walters. He's been in my unit for years, and, well, you all know Kate Jenkins."

As the group began to mingle, agent Sanchez crossed the aisle with purpose, and headed directly to Jane. "Your reputation precedes you agent Newell. I suppose I should feel honored to be on the same team as you."

Ignoring the sudden tingle in her spine, and how the frizzy hairs at the nape of her neck seemed to stand on end, Jane shook his hand. "It's nice to meet you as well, agent Sanchez."

She had been told about the bureau plane they had access to for certain cases and tried to hide her surprise when the group gravitated toward a section with bench seats on either side of a table in response to a ting they all heard coming from the laptop set in the center of it.

"Here is Abbey now, joining us via Skype," Bill told them. They all watched while their computer guru's round face, purple highlight ed coal black hair, and studded horn-rimmed glasses came into focus. With a backdrop of computer monitors and fluorescent lights, she seemed like a breath of fresh air to Jane when she heard her expressive, almost lilting voice.

"Good early morning my darling crime fighters, I just love technology. Seeing your beautiful faces helps me deal with the ick I'm about to display on the screen."

"Thanks Abs, I'll take it from here, but if you could send this to our handhelds, I'd appreciate it." Using his pencil to point out the horror, Bill went on. "The M.E. has already removed our female victim, but here are the in-situ pictures. She will explain the forensic details after she's examined her at the lab, but notable, and the reason the Michigan State Police called us in, is because of the extensive torture, and seemingly disarticulated arms. Her eyes are also taped open, and except for what look like burns on her back, we have all the signatures of not only a serial, but a copycat serial."

Seth walked closer to the screen, and added, "Wilkins left dolls with his victims, and this unidentified subject, or unsub, didn't, although she is a young mother, and the methodology is the same."

"Definitely a copycat," Sanchez interrupted, "Jane should know all about this killer. She lived with the Original Mother Killer for 15 years. She had to have an idea of his psychopathy, even before he was caught."

"So, my unique perspective could be helpful, wouldn't you agree, agent?" Jane didn't want to seem antagonistic but felt if she allowed Sanchez to get the upper hand now, she'd never get the respect of the team.

Jane noticed that Sanchez retreated quickly to his seat when he was met by the steely glares from the group.

"Stand down Agent Sanchez, we are all aware this is a copycat. Abbey is sending the Tad Wilkins file," Bill said, and then added, "Everyone should review the files, and then try to get some rest. We will need to hit the ground running once the plane lands in a little less than two hours."

Chapter Two

Day One

Mid-flight

Sanchez was aghast at how Bill introduced him as being on loan from Cyber because it made him feel like a pair of boots, not a man who should've had the field agent's spot in the unit over Jane Newell, the daughter of a damned serial killer. He was certain that her porcelain-like skin, framed by eyes the size of a full moon, and long charcoal black hair, were not only what got her into Quantico, but aided in all the damn accolades as well. Hell, she probably slept her way to the top of her class.

When Abe Alejandro, the Quantico instructor that made his own time at the Academy a living hell, sought him out seven months ago it was not to catch up with an old student. Ole Abe was always a bully and couldn't pass up the chance to rub Sanchez's nose in the fact that a girl named Jane had broken all the records at Quantico, and was now the frontrunner for a spot on the elite team led by Bill Jacobs.

That news restored the rage that had been his constant companion since his little sister, princess Lacy, hijacked all the attention and affection of his parents. He learned at a young age that females were a cunning and manipulative species who used their wiles to bend the will of everyone who came into their orbit. He schooled his family on who the superior sibling really was and knew he wouldn't hesitate to do it again in the bureau, because he was more qualified than any woman to be a field agent, and he planned, one way or another, to prove it. It would be no problem to reunite with his dark web connections if it became necessary to prove his superiority once again.

Sanchez shared his thoughts about not being considered for the position with a colleague in Cyber, Lloyd Tally, who recommended he submit a formal request for consideration on the team. Included with all the bureaucratic paperwork, Sanchez also submitted a compelling letter that listed all his accomplishments as a veteran FBI agent. He was granted an interview with Bill and the director, but in hindsight knew it was only because his paperwork was flawless, and his letter so eloquently penned. He never stood a chance at beating the woman and winning the position.

When Bill told him he thought Jane would be a better fit for the long haul, he offered Sanchez two consolation assignments. He could become a field agent, but the only opening was for a Resident Agency near The Glacier National Park in the mountains of Montana, or he could stay with Cyber, in D.C. If he stayed, Bill alluded to the idea that he could occasionally get detailed to his unit for help on a case, and while that made him feel like a minor league baseball player, he could not envision himself in a one-man office whose biggest challenge would be to find lost hikers in the snowy mountains.

Sanchez made his decision to stay with Cyber once Tally told him that his position in the unit was taken by the same Jane who'd beat his Quantico scores, and that she was the daughter of convicted serial killer, Tad Wilkins. He also implied that many of the agents at the time felt that Jane was aware of, if not a partner to, her father's kills. Once he walked off the tidal wave of bitterness at losing the position to a female with a dubious past, he had a plan of action in place. He would use his skills to dig into Jane Newell's life, and would leave no stone unturned, so that when the time was right, he'd be able to step into the spot she stole from him.

Being called up to work the copycat case seemed like divine intervention, and he felt it would be his chance to prove he was the better candidate for the spot on the team. But with the glowing introduction Bill made of her, it was clear to Sanchez that once again, the bane of his existence was going to be a female, and her name was Jane Newell.

CHAPTER THREE

DAY ONE

Mid-Air

While she had no intention of sleeping, Jane did close her eyes. She hoped she could shut down the internal alarms that Sanchez set off, by replaying their brief encounters. His bullying didn't bother her, she was used to that, so what was it, she wondered, that had her instincts pinging off all the nerve endings in her body. As she so often did when faced with an uncomfortable situation, Jane quieted her mind, and drifted back to what brought her here, and more, why she developed her perceptive instincts of others. Sanchez did have something right, though: she *was* the daughter of the original mother-killer.

Her childhood ended on the day Tad was arrested in her home by a team of SWAT and FBI agents. When they stormed her door with heavy artillery, wearing flak jackets, helmets, and goggles, to the 15-year-old girl, they looked like a bunch of bugs in a computer game, marching up an ant hill.

When the thundering boots quieted, and her father was handcuffed, she remembered the words she would spend a lifetime hearing and trying to atone for. When a solemn voice recited the names of 15 women he was being charged with abducting, torturing, and murdering, she was certain they were wrong, but when she met his eyes as they put him into a squad car, she knew there was no mistake. Instead of seeing the warm blue eyes and reassuring smile she expected, she saw a mask of hatred with eyes that looked like icy dark holes, and a crooked, almost demonic grin. When you learn that you were raised by a psychopathic serial killer, self-preservation dictates you hone your instincts, and then trust them. The feeling she had when Adrian Sanchez made eye contact may be nothing, but her therapist, Dr. Isles, as well as her aunt Judy had taught her to pay attention to those early signs of discomfort.

"Hey Jane," Kate said as she nudged her friend's elbow, "are you awake? You seem a million miles away."

Jane opened the messenger bag she wore cross body and since her coffee cup was empty, grabbed the bottle of water she knew she'd find inside.

"Yeah, I'm fine, I was just thinking about Aunt Judy. I need to text her, so she knows to check in on Charli. We left in such a hurry, I didn't leave enough food, or an extra litter box for her."

"Your cat will be fine. What else is going on in that big ass brain of yours?"

Jane trained her eyes on Kate and shook her head at how well her best friend knew her but didn't feel comfortable sharing the vibes she'd gotten from a fellow agent.

"I'm fine, really. I was just thinking about the day the monster got arrested and Aunt Judy showed up at the police station. She marched in like an army general with a war plan and was not going to be intimidated by an alphabet soup of law enforcement who were trying their hardest to connect me to that man's horrific crimes."

She knew Kate recalled it because when her Aunt Judy took the sabbatical, she was working with her at VSU in the graduate program. Kate did her thesis on how different types of psychopathy contribute to criminal behavior, and Judy was her advisor.

Jane remembered that day at the police station and how conflicted she was between the woman who took the Holly Police Department by storm, and with the aunt she hadn't seen since she was eight years old.

Her dad had told her that she dropped out of their lives because she was too busy being a hot shot college professor, and because seeing Jane brought back too many painful memories of the sister she'd lost.

Jane picked at the label on her water bottle and reflected on how long it had taken for her to believe that Aunt Judy did not abandon her at eight years old, that she was forced out of her life by her father. She began honing her instincts after Tad's arrest as the many layers he'd kept hidden began to unravel, and she never wanted to be fooled by a disingenuous person again.

She knew that her friend knew the details as well as she herself did, but appreciated that Kate sat quietly through her introspection. Jane knew how important it was, especially right now, that she be able to see it, feel it, process it, and then put it away.

"Now, after all these years, I believe that my aunt Judy picked me up and carried me until I was ready to stand on my own again. Despite my shitty attitude, she stayed by my side as my guardian, through hours and hours of interviews and psychological evaluations. As a psych professor, and bad ass in her own right, she was not going to allow anyone to build a case against me around their theories that I somehow knew what that man was up to."

"I remember how adamant she was to get permanent guardianship and approval to move you to Virginia and change your name," Kate said.

Jane smiled at that, grateful again that those changes her aunt had fought for helped her escape the notoriety of the Wilkins name. The reporters never found her, even though she spent the first couple of years looking over her shoulder for cameras and microphones.

Jane squirmed in her seat, then took another drink of water. "I'm not sure if I ever thanked her for her low key, undemanding recommendation that I get into therapy. Dr. Isles saw me through the darkest days of my life."

Jane recalled Aunt Judy's gentle tone when she told her that the choice to share her experience with a therapist, or anyone else, was entirely up to her, but she believed that her life would be far more fulfilling if she had help sorting through it all. Jane gazed out at the pre-dawn darkness from the plane's window, and acknowledged to her friend, "Those two women are the ones who helped me see the signs and signals I'd missed all those years and helped me come to terms with the fact that my own father is a psychopath, incapable of feelings, even for his own daughter."

"And look at you now," Kate declared, "you're a bad ass FBI agent despite his crazy self."

With a chuckle, Jane replied, "and as a bad ass woman now, I'm almost ashamed to admit that I didn't see the signs back then, but I'll be damned if I'm caught unaware again."

Wishing her water was a fresh cup of coffee, Jane took her hand-held out of her bag, then settled in to study the files Abbey had sent. By the time the seat belt light tinged, she decided that her intuition may or may not be accurate, but that a close eye on Adrian Sanchez was most definitely in order.

CHAPTER FOUR

DAY ONE – 7:30 AM

Oakland County, Airport – Pontiac, Michigan – 7:30 AM

With the laptop still on the table, the entire team's attention was drawn to a shrill ding alerting them to an incoming Skype, and the voice of their analyst.

"Hello crime fighting friends, I have news...bad news. No photos, but it's still really bad."

Sanchez cut in over her voice, "Just get to the point, Abbey, we just landed, and we all want off this plane."

Jane noticed Bill's stern expression when he held up his hand to silence the arrogant agent."Go ahead, Abbey. So sorry for the interruption."

"As I was trying to say, agents, the Commander from the Michigan State Police Post in Holly just called. Crime scene found another body about 1000 yards away from the first, and she's, well, fresher than the first one. The M.E. is on her way back, and they're keeping the scene intact until you arrive. I will send the coordinates to your phones. Abbey Louise out."

And with that, the computer screen went blank, and a dark pall fell over the group until Bill snapped them out of their head space with instructions.

"We have two SUVs waiting for us and have a room where we can set up our command center at the MSP post, on Dixie Highway, in Holly. Sanchez, I want you to take one of them and head over there. With what we already have, you should be able to start the case board, the rest will get filled in as we go."

Sanchez started to pipe up with a complaint about a rookie going to a crime scene when he was available, but Bill continued, "The rest of you are with me. We'll head to the scene and meet with the local PD, and get as much as we can from the M.E."

Sanchez barked as soon as Bill was finished, "why would you send a trainee with connections to the original killer, to the crime scene when I'm available?"

"You're out of line, Sanchez," Bill fired off. "Either be a part of this team, or find a way back to Quantico because I don't have time for any fragile egos. Abbey is getting Wilkins's prison records; be ready to brief us when we get back."

The remainder of the team silently de-boarded the plane and got into the waiting SUV. From her perch in the backseat, Jane's eyes followed Sanchez as he plodded his way to the other vehicle, and even with his head bowed down, she could see that his pale gray eyes were hard as ice and were zeroed in on her.

CHAPTER FIVE

DAY ONE - 7:00 AM

Ionia State Penitentiary

I'm not sure if it's the architect, or the psychopath in me, but I find it rewarding beyond belief to see something I've so carefully designed, come to fruition. Having control over another's life, and death, is my bailiwick, and has consumed my every thought for as long as I can remember. Even before my lifetime lease began in prison, I was busy on the outside preparing for when I'd have to take my games to another level. Another of my unique qualities is that I'm a visionary, so even as a free man I was prudent enough to engineer a future where, regardless of my residency, I'd be able to manipulate others. The alliances I've built inside have only been add-ons to those I built while I was still active and have made me wealthy beyond measure. So, while I may not actually be able to watch the eyes fade to the lifeless death stare I so love, I can still facilitate that moment.

I've also been kept informed on my daughter's life. Not so much because I cared about how she grew up, but because she's mine. When she was accepted into the FBI training academy at Quantico, I was furious. That she chose to work for the people who'd taken me from her and shattered my plan of molding her into my image was unforgivable, so I devised a plan to circumvent it from happening. Jane was never going to enjoy the FBI career she'd worked so hard for. The starring role she had in the script I've so brilliantly written would ensure that.

I began building my intricate cast of characters a year ago when I learned of her career path. I'm a very patient man, and as I did when I was taking young mothers, the hunting and planning was as important as the kill itself. With generous library privileges, guards on my payroll and a brilliant way to use the Dewey Decimal system to get messages outside of my prison walls, getting access to my own FBI file was the first hurdle I cleared. Knowing what the FBI knew, when they knew it, and the agents on the task force that finally brought me down was a critical component to the play I was writing.

Once I chose my protégé, I decided on an inside disciple who could facilitate my initial contact with him. Once that choice was made, I began to groom the student in preparation to be trained as the New Mother Killer. I am so good at manipulating people into thinking they're making their own decisions, that it wasn't long before he'd chosen his own underling. He didn't realize it, but his personal lackey was also handpicked by me. He was crucial to my play, because it was his role that would bring Jane into the game, and to her ultimate spiral.

I trained my protégé to accelerate his kills faster than I had, but the timing was crucial because if not perfect, Jane may not be drawn in. And drawing Jane to my doorstep would be the catalyst to my main goal – her fall from grace. And that needed to happen sooner rather than later.

Chapter Six

Day One - 7:30 AM

Oakland County International Airport

Sanchez stood by the bureau issued Expedition he'd been assigned and looked at his phone to hide his glare at Jane as she tossed her wavy hair back over her shoulder. He was bewildered over the notion that everyone else ignored the coy manner of the head tilt, or the impish grin on her face as she stepped into the vehicle. He was astounded that Bill would take a novice to what would undoubtedly be a gruesome crime scene when he, an expert was available. It made no sense, any moron could start a murder board, but it took grit to view a murder scene.

As he stepped into the truck, he silenced his phone. The incessant dinging of Abbey's incoming files was a distraction to his dark thoughts. He wished he could be with the team at the crime scene, if for no other reason than to watch Jane crumble when she witnessed the work of a killer emulating her dear old dad. Although, if what his colleague suggested was true, and she was a participant in the past deeds, then she wouldn't be shocked or get ill, but instead, might take comfort in the memory. All women have a tell, and he'd pick up that bitch's in an instant.

With the cruise control set, Sanchez's mind replayed the exchange on the airplane. His anger threatened to boil over again at the way Jane spoke to him. He thought sure the group would take issue with her being insubordinate to a ranking agent when she made the snide remark about bringing a unique perspective to the case. But instead, the steely glares were directed at him, which was more proof that he would need to up his game if he wanted to prove he was a better choice for the job. Agent Newell's fall from grace might require a nudge, which he was more than capable of providing, but meanwhile, Sanchez decided he would over-perform the tasks he was given, regardless of how menial or beneath his ability they were. Bill would realize his value once the rookie deteriorated.

The front end of the Expedition dropped with a thud as Sanchez pulled into the parking lot. He was familiar with the state's reputation for big ass potholes, he just didn't expect them in the parking lot of the Michigan State Police Post. As he stepped out of the SUV and turned his phone's ringer back on, he turned his ankle in one of the crater sized holes that was filled with water, and while he was able to regain his balance before he fell, he hoped no one saw it.

To cover his embarrassment, Sanchez shook the water off his pant leg and looked at his phone. He was glad he was still outside because hiding the excitement on his face when he read the new message could have been difficult.

We share a common dislike for a certain rookie on your team, and I have information that will help us all get what we want – to end her career before it ever gets started. If you're interested in my partnership buy an untraceable phone and respond to this text – but don't wait too long. This offer, and this phone's access will expire soon. Think about it.

Sanchez found the timing of the text oddly disturbing, but also compelling because it validated his decision to destroy Jane's career. He briefly questioned who the text could have come from, and what information they had, but he was also a pragmatic man who went after what he wanted, and he wanted Jane Newell to crash and burn, so if a partner became necessary to accomplish that goal then he'd take on a partner.

CHAPTER SEVEN

DAY ONE – 8:30AM

Rural Oakland County - Rose Township, MI

Jane knew that as realistic as Quantico's Hogan's Alley was, the real thing more than likely had a totally different feel about it. She wasn't apprehensive about crime scene protocol because she was trained for it. And she wasn't squeamish, so the sight of a dead body wasn't a big concern either. But seeing what her father's victims looked like was something she knew she'd have to work through. Even just hearing Kate's words in her head that this was an entirely new case, and not Tad's work, had a way of grounding her. Keep the cases separate, she thought, as the SUV bounced on the gravel roads. After what seemed like miles of winding dirt roads through heavily treed woods, the group of agents approached what was unmistakably their destination. They pulled over on the shoulder of the road, and parked behind a forensics van and a wagon with a County Morgue magnet on the side.

"Good morning, are you the folks from the FBI?" The badge on his Carhart jacket, and the revolver on the hip of his Wranglers, was the only visible indication that the man greeting them was law enforcement.

Bill took his outstretched hand, and said, "Yes, I'm Supervisory Special Agent Bill Jacobs, and these are agents Jenkins, Newell, and Thomas."

"Mighty glad to have you. I'm the police chief for the village of Holly, Sam Childers. We got ourselves a hell of a mess. Ain't never seen anything like it. I'm glad the State boys called you in, we need all the help we can get."

"We will use all our resources to help solve this case. Will you walk us through it?"

"I will. The first lady was found just over that hill. Follow me but be careful, it rained last night so the leaves may be a little slick."

Jane was happy that her daily footwear was sensible walking boots, unlike Kate, who, regardless of the time of day, always looked like she just stepped off a catalog cover. Her rhetorical question, "How are those heels feeling, Kate," was met with a side glance and a smirk.

After they signed in at the scene with the officer and were given gloves, they ducked underneath the tape and proceeded in silence to the painted outline that just hours before had represented a woman. Jane noticed that the others on her team were examining the thick woods outside of the taped off area, and she did the same, trusting that along with them, she'd know what she was looking for when she saw it.

"There isn't much left here to see," Kate said, "would you take us to the newest scene, Chief Childers?"

"I sure will. Dr. Maura is already up there, and it's either Sam, or just chief if you'd rather. Nothing too formal around here, and just so's you know, the young man who found her gave his statement and his contact info to Commander Murphy over to the post."

The walk to the second crime scene took the group through a tunnel of large, mature oak trees. Jane remembered how she loved hiking with friends when she was young, and how she was mesmerized by the vivid kaleidoscope of color changes in the leaves of the season. Today however, it felt like the trees' towering limbs were weeping as the spent raindrops dripped from the leaves that still clung to their branches. It was almost as if they knew the path led to a horrific display of pure evil.

The group stopped short of the scene's perimeter to take stock of the bustling activity.

"CSI seems to be doing a very thorough job," Seth commented as he retrieved a new pair of gloves from his pocket and proceeded forward. The rest of the group followed the quiet, mission-oriented agent as he led them to the taped off area.

"For sure," Jane said as she snapped her gloves at her wrist, "I did some reading about the Oakland County Crime lab on the way over, and they're considered state of the art."

"Well, hopefully our killer left a piece of himself behind," Bill added with an eye roll that indicated he knew how unlikely that was. "If it's there, I'm sure those CSI's will find it."

"And preserve it." Kate added, "Let's go introduce ourselves to the Medical Examiner."

Careful again to stay within the perimeter already processed, they side-stepped a gurney, and nodded at the assistant standing ready to help move the victim. The doctor, also in full PPE, rose from her stooped position at the body and greeted them.

"Good morning, agents, I'm Dr. Maura Hayes, the chief medical examiner in Oakland County. I can't shake your hands right now but am awfully glad to have your expertise on this case. This killer is a monster. Sam, I'm sorry I have to see you again so soon after our earlier morning trip through these woods."

The team of agents made their own introductions as they circled around the woman lying beneath a tree. Glistening wet leaves fluttered down on her as if they wanted to cover and protect the soul of a life so brutally taken.

"I can't give you definitive answers until I have her back at my lab, but I can tell you that she's been dead between 23 & 36 hours. She's starting to come out of rigor, which usually takes about 36 hours, and I can tell you that she was moved post-mortem because of this." The Dr. paused to roll her on to her side and continued, "see this purplish-blue along her side? That is where her blood pooled after she died, which would indicate she died lying on her left side, and we found her on her back." The agents nodded in understanding as she gently rolled her back.

Bill looked at the carpet of wet leaves around the scene, and said, "impossible to see any tracks, but the unidentified subject, or unsub, had to have transported them somehow and it's clear that a vehicle couldn't get here, so we'll want to check ownership records for Gators, or even a 4X4."

"Foliage truly is a killer's dream come true," Seth added, "it's the natural forensic countermeasure."

Jane knew she was being watched by the team for any sign of mental stress, but aside from being deeply saddened, she felt solid – no visions or images of her father's maniacal grin invaded her thoughts. This truly was a whole new case, and when she looked down at the open, fixed, and lifeless eyes of the young woman, the rage inside only strengthened her determination to cage this monster.

"Do you see here," the M.E. asked while lifting her arm, "like the first victim, it appears as if her shoulders have been pulled out of their sockets. I am betting that I'll find ripped or stretched tendons when I do the autopsies."

"Just like the Mother Killer did," Jane said, and added when the rest of the team looked at her in surprise, "Don't look so flabbergasted, I've studied his cases, too."

"Are those contusions around her neck?" Seth asked.

"Yes, this slight hemorrhage in the capillaries of her eyes is petechia, and I'll confirm it at the lab, but strangulation is more than likely the cause of death." She asked her assistant, Stan, to help roll her on to her stomach, then went on, "These marks on her back look almost like your killer was trying to burn some sort of crude design into her skin. The first victim has them as well, so I'll compare them when I get her on my table. The inflammation and abscessing of the wounds indicate they were made anti-mortem."

The angry blistering around the wounds made it clear that this young lady suffered a great deal before she died. Seth stepped back from the body, and said, "So, burns on both of the bodies could be this unsub's signature."

As the training agent in the field, Kate looked to Jane and explained that the signature is something a killer has to do for himself but doesn't really have anything to do with the actual act of killing.

"Methodology," she concluded, "is the way they torture and kill, and these two women were killed and tortured in the same way as the mother killer did. Neither his signature, nor his methodology was ever made public."

Jane nodded her understanding, and then asked, "Have you been able to ID either of them yet, Doctor?" She felt it was important to humanize them rather than referring to them as just victims one and two.

"Not yet. Sam did provide me with the names, and toothbrushes of women reported missing in his town in the last week."

"Yep," Sam interjected, "Allison Broux, age 25 was reported missing by her husband, John, seven days ago, and Mandy Leonard, also 25, has been missing about four days according to her husband, Joseph. I figured you'd be able to get DNA from the toothbrushes."

Impressed with his forethought, Kate said, "Good thinking, Sam, and we can have our analyst expand the search, if necessary." She then turned to Dr. Maura and asked, "Any idea how long it'll take to check for a match, or when you might get to the autopsies?"

"Stan and I are ready to get her back to the morgue now and they both have priority, so I'll be getting to work on them right away. If you want, you can plan on meeting with me at the lab in about three hours. I'm sure I'll have more information for you by then."

"That sounds like a solid plan," Kate said. "We'll head to the command center and meet with the task force for now and will see you in a little while." Kate asked the doctor for her phone number, and then sent her a text so they'd have contact information for each other.

Jane spent her walk back through the woods quietly processing what she'd seen and heard. As personally committed as she was to caging monsters, she also knew she was being observed. It was her opportunity, as Kate put it, to kick some ass and prove she was worthy of being a part of an elite team, and she was steadfastly resolved to contribute and prove her mettle.

When they pulled into the unpaved parking lot of the Michigan State Police Post, Jane noticed the virtual minefield of rock-filled puddles, and couldn't help ribbing her friend: "Do they make rubber shoe covers with spiked heels? You could sure use some right about now."

Kate gave Jane a mocking sneer, and as they opened the door, Seth, showing an uncharacteristic sense of humor, added, "They'd be a good thing to pack in your ready bag."

They were met at the door by the commander of the post, and his imposing presence seemed to match his rank. Jane would describe him as Navy Seal big, yet with his closely cropped white hair, creamy Irish complexion and sapphire blue eyes, his intimidation factor was low on the scale. Of course, they were meeting him in an at-ease situation, and Jane was certain he could intimidate and kick ass if it was needed.

"Good morning, I'm Commander, Patrick Murphy. Thanks for organizing this task force. Your agent is in the incident room. I see Sam is pulling into the parking lot now, so let's grab some coffee and go see what we've got so far."

As they navigated their way single file through the narrow hallway, Jane exchanged nods and friendly smiles with the officers and staff, and followed her nose to the smell of fresh coffee. She'd heard that cop shop coffee was like crude motor oil, but what she smelled felt like a blissful awakening to pure nirvana. She also noticed how Kate lagged just long enough to share conversation on the short walk, with the very handsome Patrick Murphy.

"Hey, Sanchez," Bill said as he entered the room, "good start on the whiteboard. Hopefully we'll have names to add by this evening."

Sanchez nodded at Bill, but with the tension and tautness in his rigid stance, and the side eye glare directed her way, Jane sensed that it wasn't Bill he was tuned into. The cold shivers up her back snapped her mind back to the room, and the case. She could not allow her gut reaction to Sanchez's authenticity or motives interfere with the job because she knew he'd sense her vulnerability and wouldn't hesitate to use it against her.

While Sam gave his report, and shared information on the two women recently reported missing, Jane put her mind in check at how she reacted to seeing Sanchez. She was sure he noticed the sudden shift in her demeanor, and she could not allow that to happen. Without a willingness to share her unease about him with Kate, she knew she'd have to navigate her own way through the angst.

"So, if everyone is in agreement," Jane tuned back into Sam's voice, "and these young ladies are the ones that've gone missing, I'd like to tell their husbands."

Jane guessed that she was not alone in the newfound respect she felt for Sam at volunteering to make the notification because she knew it was the hardest part of a cop's job.

"This is my town, and these are my folks. I think it's only right that I take the time to deliver the news."

All eyes went to the front of the room when the computer Sanchez had been working on sent out a loud, shrill ring.

"I connected the computer to the big screen on the wall. That'll be Abbey with Wilkins's prison information. Even you in the back of the room will be able to see her." Jane did not miss how his dispassionate eyes bored into her like lasers with that remark.

"Good afternoon, how are my ambassadors for all that is good? And hello, also, to my new crime fighting friends." Without even seeming to try, Abbey's musical voice brought just a little brightness to the darkness they'd all seen that day, but Jane wasn't too surprised to see how Sanchez's body seemed to tense up.

"Ok, this may come as a surprise, but Tad Wilkins behaves like a model prisoner. It seems when his lifetime charter, courtesy of the great State of Michigan first began, he built his reputation as being nutty as a fruitcake, so even the meanest of the jailbirds didn't mess with him."

"Abs, how about visitors, and does he have a prison job?" Seth asked.

"There is no record of him getting a visitor, or mail, but he did have a cellmate, Luke Johnson, who routinely got both. Johnson's lawyer, Sal Faraci, who according to the word in the yard is connected, and a Tonya Baxter, listed as his ex-wife, also visited. Johnson was released about six months ago. Oh, and Wilkins works in the kitchen."

"Ok, well he has to be communicating with someone on the outside," Kate said, "these two new kills have characteristics that were never made public."

"We're going to need to talk to those three. Abs, will you..." but before Bill could continue she answered: "I've already started the dive on all three of them, and will get you that information, and their contact info as soon as I have it. All for now, lovelies, Abbey Louise out."

Jane wondered if anyone else caught Sanchez's eye roll as the wall screen went blank, but then turned toward Patrick's commanding voice when he told them he'd reserved rooms for them at a Quality Inn about eight miles away. They still had a couple of hours before their meeting with Dr. Maura, and there wasn't much they could do until the bodies were identified, so the team decided to get checked into their rooms.

Bill addressed Kate, "you three get yourselves checked in, Seth and I are going to stay back and go over the statement from the guy who found our first body." Kate nodded as he continued, "Kate and Jane, go ahead and meet with the M.E. when she's ready, and then head back to the post. Sanchez, you can ride back in with Seth and I. If we leave around 4:00, it should give us time to grab dinner and be back for a 5:30 briefing."

Jane wasn't particularly pleased with having Sanchez in their car for the ride to the hotel but stowed the feeling as they headed out. Kate's sudden halt stopped them at the door.

"I'm going to go tell Commander Murphy our plans to meet back here at 5:30."

Jane grinned at her friend's obvious attraction, and as she headed toward the driver's seat of their vehicle, it occurred to her that it had been a long time since she'd seen Kate's head turn toward a man. It was painfully clear that her friend had insulated herself from the affection of the opposite sex, and while Jane suspected she knew the underlying reason, it was a part of herself that Kate kept closed off, and she had too much respect for her to push.

CHAPTER EIGHT

DAY ONE

In the back seat, Sanchez's resentment reached a whole new level when he thought of how the agents walked into the incident center like they were the all-star team with their game plan already set. He'd done great work setting up the live chat on the big screen, yet no one seemed to acknowledge it. It would've been just as easy to print the information from Abbey and pass it out, but he thought if he went above and beyond setting up the board, that Bill and the others would realize that his talents were being wasted. He did have his first smile of the day, however, when he remembered how the princess rookie's demeanor went from a self-assured, engaged agent, to a deer, frozen still in headlights when she saw him.

With his mirrored, aviator sunglasses, Sanchez was able to stare into Jane's back undetected, and imagined her squirming under his laser focused glare. His sudden realization that nothing he did would gain him favor over Jane, rocketed him to another level of fury. Being bested by a female was unacceptable, and when that female was Jane Newell, it was downright absurd. Sanchez's indignation at that thought reaffirmed his determination to torpedo her career.

"Hey ladies," he said in his nice voice, "will you stop at that liquor store on the right? I want to get a bottle."

Sanchez was happy the store sold burner flip phones because his idea to annihilate Jane's career just became a certainty, and since he felt as invisible as a piece of cellophane, he decided he could text his anonymous ally from the backseat.

I'm in – let's do this.

CHAPTER NINE

DAY ONE- 3:00 PM

Oakland County Medical Examiner's Building

Jane tossed what remained of her Burger King Whopper into the empty bag and took a final drink of her coffee before stepping out of the car.

"I'm not crazy about fast food, but that hit the spot. It's been a long time since my breakfast yogurt."

"Yeah, well, that notion you have of your body being a sanctuary for only wholesome goodness, and of course coffee, will become more and more unrealistic the longer you're on the job," Kate told her. "You need to eat when you can, and sleep when you're able because an active case sometimes leaves precious little time for either. You ready for your first autopsy?"

"Of course," Jane answered with a confidence she wasn't sure she really had. "We observed a couple at the academy."

Kate offered a knowing smile and stepped back for Jane to enter the building. Knowing she was under observation, Jane kept her face as neutral as she could when she was assailed with the thick smell of ammonia mixed with what she could only assume was death.

"Girl, the differences between this and an academy sponsored autopsy have only just begun, so buckle up." Jane took a deep breath and proceeded to the reception desk.

"Good afternoon, I'm Agent Newell, and this is Supervisory Special Agent, Jenkins. I believe Dr. Hayes is expecting us."

"Yes, she's waiting for you in autopsy suite one. Please sign in and come through, it's the second door on the right. You will find paper gowns, skull caps for your hair, and booties through the first door. Please put it all on before you enter the suite."

While Jane was getting into her PPE, she looked through a window into what looked like a room made entirely of stainless steel. With her back to them, the Medical Examiner was facing a wall paneled with what looked like six individual drawers with handles. When she saw their reflection in the shiny stainless backdrop, she turned around and gestured them in.

"Does your thick head of curls fit into that cap?" Jane asked as she rummaged through her bag, "I don't think I can get all of mine up into it."

"Yes, mine will fit, but don't you have a scrunchie in that messenger bag you always have strapped to your chest?" Jane smiled, and having found the coveted hair tie, secured it all in a high ponytail before putting on the cap.

Stepping into the room, Kate greeted the M.E. "Hi, Doctor, thanks for meeting with us so quickly. Your text said you had a few things to show us?"

"I do, and if you call me Maura, I'll call you by your first names. The titles are fine in the field, or for introductions, but when you're sharing the gruesome, horrific things that one human can inflict on another, well, that's pretty personal."

"Thank you, Maura, and we agree. First, have you by chance been able to match their ID to the samples Sam brought you?"

"Yes, I was," Maura said as she walked past the metal gurney in the middle of the room and opened one of the cold storage drawers from the paneled wall. "The young lady you just passed is Allison Broux, and was the first victim found, and this young lady," she continued as she pulled the drawer out and transferred the draped body to a wheeled gurney, "is Mandy Leonard."

While Maura was occupied with the wheel locking mechanism that would hold the platform steady, Kate sent off a quick text to Bill that the ID's had been verified. Sam would visit the family to deliver the devastating news.

Jane slowly stepped up to view the women who, were it not for the gray color of death, would look as if they'd been tucked in for their slumber with a white sheet, pressed and folded beneath their chins. She was thankful for their positive identification, and although it felt like a solemn moment, she knew the only way to help Allison and Mandy now, was to find the monster responsible. Learning everything she could in here was a very important step toward that, and toward a vow she'd made 13 years ago.

"Ok, first I want to show you the X-rays. They both have the same extensive trauma, and I want to point it out because they're almost identical to the Wilkins cases." Jane caught Kate's quick glance in her direction but remained zeroed in on Maura's description. She had studied the carnage her father left in his wake but didn't want her expressions to show how she felt seeing it firsthand. Viewing the torture these women suffered was far more heartbreaking than reading the case file, and much more graphic than looking at the crime scene photos.

"See here how the tendons and the muscles in the shoulders are torn? That's most likely from being stretched to their breaking point over the course of multiple days. Also note down here at the hips, they have complete tears to their two glutenous tendons that attach to the outer aspect of the hip. A certain amount of tearing happens naturally, but they usually remain attached to the bone. This complete tear indicates repetitive injury."

"What do you think caused those injuries? They look horribly painful, but not exactly life threatening," Kate asked.

"Oh, it isn't what killed them, but if you step over to their bodies, I can show you what I've come up with." The agents joined Maura, and she continued, "The abrasions and angry red rings on their ankles and wrists indicate they were restrained with, and most certainly struggled against zip ties. I was also able to collect some minute traces of a yellow fiber. It's been sent down to the lab, but based on their condition, I think their hands were restrained behind them, and then with a yellow rope, their wrists were attached to the restraints on their ankles, which is also what the M.E. on the Wilkins victims determined." Both agents grimaced, but the doctor continued her forensic detailing.

Jane and Kate were as in tune with Maura's body demonstration as they were with her words.

"I didn't show you, but the X-rays also indicate traumatic lesions to the Clivus, which is a tiny spot above the C-1 cervical bone at the top of the neck. So, picture yourself hogtied, and how your back is forcefully arched so that your wrists and ankles are close enough to be tied together. Now, if you're forced to hold that position for any length of time, what do you think is going to happen to your head, your neck and even your hip bones?"

The way Maura's back arched when she raised her chin and pressed her shoulders back, provided the ladies with a clear visual aid of what these women endured.

Jane exhaled a breath she didn't even realize she was holding, and whispered to what she thought was just herself, "Holy shit."

"You got that right," Kate said with a shake of her head, "these poor women. I studied the Wilkins file, too, but seeing it in the flesh is totally different. This maniac must be stopped."

"I'm going to turn them over and show you the deviation from Wilkins' victims."

Jane and Kate didn't even try to hide the horror on their faces, or their audible gasps when they looked at the women's backs. The raised welts, swabbed clean since the crime scene, looked even more like a mutant ghoul trying to communicate with a flaming crimson tongue.

"Those burns were made by a very hot, pointed object. Before they died."

"Like a fireplace poker, maybe?" Jane asked.

"Possibly, but on our first victim, Allison, there are what look like three crudely drawn circles, and on Mandy, there are five." Maura pointed out the marks with a surgical pointer, and concluded, "see how there are three on top, and then two down below it?"

"It may be nothing," Jane said as she snapped a picture with her phone, "but it's entirely different from anything Wilkins did. I'll send these over to Abbey to search the system for other cases with this signature."

"Great idea, rookie. What else can you tell us, Maura?"

"The official cause of death is strangulation. The multiple abrasions, and the variations in color on the bruises around them indicate they were strangled several times, over the course of a few days before they died."

Kate adjusted her cap, and said "Yeah, to this crazy unsub, that's just another fun way to torture them. Tape their eyes open so they have to watch, then strangle them until they lose consciousness, and then revive them. It allows him the pleasure of doing it again. This guy gets off on the torture, probably more than the actual kill. I'm guessing, like the Wilkins victims, there is no sign of sexual assault?"

"No signs of sexual assault on either one of them. I did find some of what looks like the same rope fibers from around each of their wrists, embedded in their necks. It's also been sent to the lab, and if you find a spool of rope, we will be able to match it. I scraped the adhesive residue from the tape that held their eyes open, but like Wilkins' victims, it appears to be ordinary duct tape: easy to find, impossible to trace." The agents followed her back to the changing room, and Maura continued.

"I've sent my report to Patrick, so your team will have it when you get back, but based on body temp, decomp, and some scavenger activity, Allison had been dead about four days, and Mandy, just about 30 hours when they were found."

"Have you run the toxicology yet?" Jane asked, "or was anything present that might indicate how he was able to subdue them? I'm pretty sure they didn't just hop in a car with him."

"Good question, Jane. There were no sedatives in their systems, but I did notice that above both of their lips there appeared to be a rash, or some sort of irritation, so I took some scrapings, and sent them to the lab. If he's dosing them with some form of ether, it's my opinion that he's doing it multiple times, probably to subdue them during the burning stage of the torture."

As the three women put their PPE in the medical refuse container, Kate thanked Maura again for expediting the examinations.

"Just catch this son of a bitch so he doesn't do it again," she told them. "I'll text you once I get the labs back."

Jane and Kate shared a silent walk back to the car, quietly absorbing all they'd seen. Jane learned at a very young age that monsters truly did exist, but after seeing their work with her own eyes, she was forced to believe what, to most, is unbelievable.

"Are you ever able to un-see something like that?" Jane asked once they hit the highway.

"Well, the short answer is yes, but no, and what I mean by that is, the images of Allison and Mandy may fade over time, but there will always be another morgue and another medical examiner to forensically detail just how depraved and evil some humans are."

"I'd like to say that I'm sorry I ever laid eyes on that, or that I should've been a psychologist like Aunt Judy, but I can't. Is it horrible that even after seeing what we just saw that I am more committed than ever to doing this job, and being the best at it? Not only do I want a piece of this asshat, but I also want a piece of every scumbag predator out there."

Kate looked at Jane, and smiled with her reply, "not at all, rookie. It makes you perfect for this job, and more, it proves that I was spot on with my assessment of you when your aunt introduced us six years ago."

"Thanks, Kate. I appreciate your insight and advice, but I have one more quick question before we walk in for our briefing. Has the smell that has permeated my nostrils, also been absorbed by my hair and clothes, and will it ever go away?"

Kate laughed as they opened the door to the police post and answered, "Well, let's just say that you should be thankful you left your precious messenger bag in the dressing room."

Jane turned her head to question her friend about that statement but was met inside the reception area by Patrick.

"Perfect timing, ladies. The coffee is fresh, and everyone is waiting in the incident room." Jane did not miss the complete smile on her friend's face as they fell into line behind the Commander.

"Don't worry," she whispered, "your lipstick looks as good as it did when you put it on at 5:00 AM." Jane was amazed that Kate, with the honeyed complexion of her bi-racial heritage and roasted almond eyes, always looked like she'd just finished primping, even when she was twelve hours into a day that she had only thirty minutes to prepare.

Jane stopped for fresh coffee, and when she walked into the incident room inhaled the steam and calmed herself with the rich, heady aroma in an attempt to shake off the apprehension she felt at being near Sanchez again. He's a member of an elite FBI team, she reprimanded herself, get over it. He's harmless.

"Welcome back everyone," Bill said from the front of the room, "at your seats you should all have the M.E.'s report. Kate and Jane will go over it in a few minutes, but let's start with Sam, who has made the family notifications."

"Thanks, Bill. Well, I have to say that was harder than anything I've ever had to do. Both John and Joe knew I was coming, so they had their parents, and their wives' parents there. Honestly, I was glad they had someone because they were real shook up."

Jane noticed that Sanchez's face lacked the look of compassion the rest of the room had when Sam went on.

"Ain't neither one of them seen anything strange recently. They both have six-month-old babies, so their routines were pretty set. Allison jogged every morning after the baby's first bottle, so John could watch him before he left for work. And Mandy, now she would alternate her days between a jog early in the morning, and a yoga class in the evening time on Mondays and Fridays."

"It says in the report," Seth added, "that Allison never came home from her jog last Tuesday, and that Mandy didn't come home after her yoga class on Friday night. Have your officers checked the yoga studio for any security cameras or anything?"

"Yep, they did that Saturday morning, but there weren't no cameras. It's just a lady from town who runs the classes in her basement. I told the husbands that the FBI was helping us, and to expect a call."

Kate walked up to the case board and added their victims' names to the timeline Sanchez had started. "Based on this timeline, and Maura's report, I think it's safe to say that he tortures them for three days before he kills and dumps them."

"That sounds about right, Kate," Bill said. "Seth and I spoke with the first responders, and the gentleman who found the first body, but none of them saw anything out of the ordinary."

A sudden energy seemed to fill the room when the door burst open and the officer they'd seen manning the entry area, ran breathless into the room.

"A man just walked in with a baby on his hip and said his wife never came home from her aerobics class. He's waiting in your office, Commander."

Bill and Seth both shot up from their seats, and as they headed for the door, Bill barked the next assignments.

"Seth and I will sit in with Patrick. Kate and Jane, take Sanchez with you, he can try to canvass the neighbors that weren't home on the first go around while you two speak with the husbands. It's getting late, so let's plan on meeting tomorrow morning at 8:00."

As Patrick bolted toward the door, he told them that their hotel offered a free continental breakfast, but that there was a Coney Island nearby that opened early.

Jane silently chided herself for feeling happy that Sanchez automatically climbed into the backseat. It was easier for her to put the unnerving feelings of distrust she had into a closed compartment if she didn't have to look at him.

As they drove through the village, Jane was reminded of how captivated she always was with the historically honest appeal of the buildings that lined the narrow streets. Tonight, however, the glowing railroad signal was the only source of light to break the total darkness that felt predictive of the dire circumstances that brought them there. And the thought that there was more than likely another woman enduring unthinkable agony had her already scattered brain twirling like a spun top.

"It's getting pretty late, and their houses are both dark." Kate said as she turned off Saginaw Street, and headed toward the homes of their victims. "Do you think we should wait until morning?"

Jane took a pack of gum out of her messenger bag, and replied, "These families have just had the worst day of their lives, and I'd hate to intrude if they're lucky enough to be resting. Maybe we should call Bill and discuss putting this off until morning."

Kate took the stick of Trident and sent a text to their boss.

"Bill and Seth are still with the gentleman who came in before we left, but he agrees with the late hour. I think I'm going to grab a vending machine sandwich from the hotel and eat it in bed after I've showered the morgue off myself. How about you guys?"

"I'm going to hit the gym, then the shower. I don't have much of an appetite, so I'm going to raid my stash of nuts and granola, text Aunt Judy, and then I'll hit the hay." Jane grimaced, then added, "Nothing packaged that comes out of a vending machine is ever good."

"Okay, girl, enjoy the bird food. How about you Sanchez? Need us to stop anywhere on the way back?"

"No, I'm good. I'm going to have a stiff drink or three, and then call it a day."

Once in her room, Jane wasted no time getting out of the khakis, V-neck tee, tank top and blazer she wore for work. It was a durable, low maintenance wardrobe that she could change the look of simply with a different color tee and tank top combo. Her blazers were mostly black, so they matched everything, and best of all, her foot-friendly boots fit well under the khakis. Swapping out the work attire for workout wear and replacing the boots for her cross-trainers boosted her pre-workout adrenaline.

Before tossing her bag on the bed, Jane plugged in her phone, put a room key in her pocket, and headed for the fitness center feeling an almost happy exhaustion after the first day on her first case. As horrifying, and unforgettable as the crime scene and morgue memories were, she was more certain than ever that she was exactly where she belonged and couldn't wait to talk with Aunt Judy about it all.

As she hit her groove on the treadmill, she smiled as she remembered some of the stories Aunt Judy told her about her mother, Hannah.

"She was smart, beautiful, and vivacious," Aunt Judy would say, "and everyone loved her. She had a special way of making other people love and be happy about who they were."

Jane smiled when she remembered how Aunt Judy tried to hide her sexual preference when she was younger, and she, not wanting to make her aunt uncomfortable, pretended she didn't know she was a lesbian. As the treadmill slowed, Jane fondly recalled their Wednesday movie nights and how very little of the chosen show they actually watched. Mostly it was their time to connect and talk, so Jane used one of those nights to reveal to her aunt that she was aware of her life partner, and all that mattered was that she was happy. She stepped off the treadmill feeling the love and commitment her aunt had made to her, and how she'd kept the personal side of her life away from Jane. She didn't want her niece to have to deal with more embarrassment, or shame, than she already had at being the daughter of a serial killer, but in truth, there is nothing Judy could have done that would've changed how she felt about her.

Jane glanced up from her final stretch, and despite the sweat she'd worked up, felt an icy chill creep up her back and into her neck when she saw who she thought was Sanchez lurking outside the room. By the time she'd toweled off and left the room, he was nowhere to be found, which had her questioning whether she had actually seen him, or if the compartment she'd set up for her Sanchez intuitions was leaking into her active brain. Easy enough to shut that door again, she thought as she rode the elevator back to her room for a much needed shower.

Jane wrapped her hair in a towel, and after putting on her giant VSU sleep shirt, grabbed a bottle of water, and sat down on her bed. Her thick mane of hair needed some towel time before she could brush it out and lay down, so she grabbed her phone and decided to text her aunt, and then review what she had on the case before calling it a night.

When she noticed a new text alert on her phone, Jane's heart felt a little happier thinking Aunt Judy probably texted to say good night, but when she unlocked her phone and read the message, her heart began to pound so hard she was afraid her ribs might splinter. Her breathing felt ragged, and her whole body felt numb after she read the message.

I know your secrets, Janey, and I know you were daddy's little helper. Are you helping now, too? Talk to you soon!

Jane planted her feet flat on the floor, and with her head between her legs forced life-giving oxygen to her brain. She knew she needed a clear head to process the message and figured, or was at least hopeful, that the reporters following this copycat case somehow connected her to Tad. She also wondered where and how they learned about the name only her father ever used, because aside from Aunt Judy and Dr. Isles, no one knew he used that pet-name.

As she brushed out her hair, Jane remembered that there was another person who knew what Tad called her but discounted it without much thought because she was certain Nick wasn't responsible.

Nick Richards was the man Jane thought she'd be with for the rest of her life. She met him during her 3rd year at VSU, and he was everything her father wasn't. He was kind and gentle, genuine, compassionate, and had a way of making Jane feel comfortable opening up and revealing things she'd only ever spoken with Dr. Isles about. When she told him how she cringed when she thought about her father calling her *Janey,* he held her cheeks in the palm of his hands and reassured her that she was not defined by what that monster did, or the names he used for her.

Admittedly, the breakup was both unexpected and contentious when she announced that she'd been accepted at Quantico. He was adamantly against her joining the bureau, yet gave her no suitable reason for why other than he was worried about her safety. She'd been an avid body builder since she was 16 years old and told him not to worry because she could kick his ass. Jane also told him that she could not be with a man who didn't support her in her dreams. Those were the last words they'd shared, but even with that, she did not think he would try to hurt her in that way. She'd moved on to her dream of becoming an FBI agent, and the last she'd heard, he had settled comfortably into the fast paced life of a financial whiz in Manhattan.

CHAPTER TEN

DAY ONE – 11:00 PM

Rural Oakland County

The news is reporting that the FBI has been called in to help solve the recent murders in Holly. Well, of course they've been called in, that was the plan. The Original Mother Killer, or OMK as I call him, had it planned since the beginning, and with the sweet Eve Laraby writhing like a fish on pavement in the back of my van, I feel very worthy of being the chosen one. The media even gave me a moniker, New Mother Killer, or NMK, and ever since my mentor started contacting me six months ago, I feel like, at 58 years old, I'm finally living my best life.

The first time the bedraggled vagrant knocked on my door, I stepped out on to the porch and shut the door behind me. I didn't want any stench from his filthy clothes and obvious lack of hygiene to invade my home. The stranger took a step backward, nearly falling off the porch, and held his hands up in surrender.

I could feel the growl in my own throat when I asked, "Who are you, and what the hell do you want?" I could see his adam's apple roll up and down in his gaunt throat as he swallowed hard and extended his arm toward me. As emaciated as he looked, I knew he was no physical threat, so I took what turned out to be an old school flip phone out of his hand.

The stranger's taught stance immediately began to loosen, and I could see his muscles relax once his hand was empty. As he lifted his chin and looked at me squarely for the first time since his arrival, he said, "You've been chosen." As he walked away from my house, he turned back and said, "He said it's your turn to be seen, and he can make it happen, but you must answer his call."

I may have been in disbelief that Tad Wilkins, the object of my secret affection and obsession for so many years was reaching out to me, but I wasn't really because it was clearly serendipitous. A lesser man may have blamed him for the debacle that became his life after the brief encounter they shared after his arrest, but to me, getting to know him became a passionate outlet for me at a time when I felt otherwise invisible. And during those moments when I felt dispirited and morose at my exiled existence, all I had to do was visualize how we connected with just one look. His deep blue eyes, and crooked grin, while shuddersome to most, was almost cathartic to me, so his reaching out with an email address and password, was unquestionably kismet.

I followed his instructions, and looked forward to logging on twice a week, always with a new ID and password, to access the letters he'd written and saved to a draft folder. I was surprised at what he knew about my life and my job and felt privileged when he confided things to me that even with my extensive research, I did not know. I learned the nickname he had for his daughter and shared his disappointment that he wasn't able to teach and mold her into the killing partner he so richly deserved, and I shared his anger when he told me she was on a path to becoming an FBI agent. He even described what he referred to as his practice kills - the ones no one would ever connect to him - and knowing him as well as I did, understood when he recommended that I also do some practicing.

I was honored and excited when he told me I was the perfect man to continue his work, and then suggested I plant a few seeds of my own to get me started before the real training began. I knew I'd pleased him, and when the same straggly man appeared at my door with a set of keys, a plat map of vacant land, and GPS coordinates to property in Michigan, I was thrilled that my real training as the OMK's protégé was about to begin. I retired the next day, packed up all my computer equipment and drove off without ever looking in my rearview mirror.

A thud and muffled moan drew my attention back to my newest playmate. The fun really began for me in these first few minutes of wakefulness when the young mothers realize they're in trouble, but still have fire in their eyes, a fighting spirit and hope. Already I can see the blood oozing from her wrists and ankles from her struggles against the zip ties for a freedom she'll never know again.

"Darling Eve, you should save your strength. Our game has just begun. Preserve some of that fight for later. You're going to need it."

Chapter 11

Day Two - 8:00 AM

Incident room – Michigan State Police Post

Bill's greeting, while friendly, seemed more like a call to arms: "I hope you all got some rest, and a hearty breakfast. We need to tug hard at every thread today, and find a way to connect some puzzle pieces." Then pointing to the timeline on the whiteboard, he added, "If this unsub holds true to form, our third victim, Eve Laraby, only has one day left."

Seemingly in sync with Bill's statement, Abbey's image came into view on the big screen. "Good morning my conquerors of evil, I have the contact information on Tad's cellmate, and his visitors. It's coming to you now." Twirling her feather topped ink pen through her jeweled fingernails, Abbey added, "I always find it interesting that ex-convicts think they're smart enough to live outside the grid, but I guess they've never run into someone with my super cyber skills"

With a chuckle, Kate asked her, "Abs, the M.E. found residue of ethyl alcohol and sulphuric acid in scrapings she took from above the victim's lips and said they're both components of ether. Is there a way you can track down where and how it can be obtained?"

"Oh, my sweet, law-abiding agent, it can't be bought, but it can be made, and if you get the mixture right, the vapors can knock a person out quicker than a ninja."

"Thanks Abs," Seth said. "Stay nearby, we may need you later."

"Abbey Louise Harris, cyber sleuth extraordinaire, at your service. Talk soon, Abbey out."

"Ok, team," Bill instructed once the call was disconnected, "I want Kate and Jane to track down Tonya Baxter and see what she knows about Wilkins's relationship with her ex, and then drive the routes our victims may have taken. See if you can find a possible abduction site and then go talk to the Leonard and Broux families."

The ladies nodded, and he continued, "Seth and I will track down the cellmate, Luke Johnson, and his attorney. Sanchez, you ride with Sam and talk to Kyle Laraby. Find out as much about his wife's routine as possible. There may be something to connect the three besides their six-month-old babies, and it wouldn't hurt to canvass the neighbors again, maybe someone has remembered something."

As the group was packing up their bags, Jane watched Sanchez's body language, and it did not look happy, but she put it aside, and addressed the group.

"Do you think it'd be worth it to have Abbey do a dive into the disposal site? I realize it's State Land, but to have put them both so close together, I'm wondering if the property holds any significance to our unsub."

"I think that's a great idea," Seth offered, and added as he opened the laptop to connect to their analyst, "if nothing else, it's another line to tug."

"I knew you couldn't stay away for long. What kind of magic can I work for you?"

Seth explained what they needed, and with her troll-topped pen between her teeth, Abbey replied, "There are over 4 million acres of State Land in Michigan, and about 3.9 of them are forested. I do love a challenge though, I'll hit you back when I have your answers. Abbey out."

CHAPTER 12

DAY TWO - 6:00 AM

Ionia State Penitentiary

So far, I have to say that my play is acting out exactly as I wrote it, and everyone seems to be playing their part as scripted. I'm not real pleased that my protégé has developed a signature of his own, but in a way I understand. I chose him to be my disciple because I sensed he felt unseen and undervalued. Being exiled as he was after my capture, I knew he'd be a perfect candidate to resume my reign of terror, and in the process, I felt good at helping another man find his true calling. But killing is a very personal experience, and it makes sense that he would want to find his own way. He has followed my instruction enough that the authorities realize that it's me, reincarnated, so I guess for now that's good enough. I'll be cutting him loose when I've gotten all I want out of him anyway, so the least I can do is to allow him to develop something of his own.

My messenger boy, Luke, despite his drug addled brain, and the sleaze bag lawyer I chose, have even met my expectations. The timing was perfect with the finding of the first two women, because as I suspected, the FBI's elite team was called in, and because of who her training agent is, Jane is on that team.

With enough money, or the threat of harm, it's relatively simple to get people in line. The guards, the company that delivers food, and the wrinkled old man in the library who allowed me access to, and showed me how to use disposable email domains that are almost impossible to track, are all beholden to me in one way or another. I would like to see Jane deteriorate quickly, though; even more, I guess I'd like to see Jane. That'll move her downfall along. I'll need to help facilitate that visit sooner rather than later.

CHAPTER 13

DAY TWO - 8:30 AM

The Village of Holly, Michigan

Sanchez knew his blood pressure was high because he could feel his heart pumping through the pulse points on his neck. He did not understand why he would be paired up with a sheriff from bum funk nowhere, and what the hell was up with all the fawning over Abbey? His cyber skills were just as good; hell, he felt like searching the land records on his own, just to show them how valuable he could be to this group of misfits.

Fucking Jane and her ideas, he thought, then took some comfort in knowing that with the help of his anonymous friend, she'd be going down soon. He was anxious to get the information he was assured would ruin her career, but for now resigned himself to playing the game just a little longer. Sanchez was aware of Sam's incessant chatter about how he felt he'd failed to protect his people but chose to ignore it. Helping Sam to cope with his miserable failings was definitely not on his list for the day.

When he felt a vibrate in his right pocket, Sanchez knew it was his burner, and with Sam still chattering away, he figured all he had to do was nod and say, "uh huh" occasionally, and he'd be able to read his new message.

Our leader is going to get impatient if we don't move things along. To that end, I'm not trusting you to compose a new message on your own. This is what needs to be said- verbatim:

I am as close to proving your involvement and bringing you down as darling Eve Laraby is to dying. Am I in your head, Janey?

Sanchez had no idea who the leader was, but complied, and sent the message.

CHAPTER 14

DAY TWO - 8:30 AM

Pontiac, Michigan

Seth and Bill could see how decades of poverty had contributed to the decay in the neighborhoods when they crossed over into the north end of Pontiac. The bustling commerce section at the city's center seemed to end from one crosswalk to the next as they traveled farther north on Woodward Ave, toward the address Abbey found for Luke Johnson. The art-deco, architecturally unique buildings were replaced with graphically tagged squat, bunker-type concrete buildings that sold liquor at state minimum prices, and individual cigarettes for a buck each.

Seth pointed to a duplex on the right and told Bill, "That must be the place."

"You mean the one with the blue tarp over half the roof?" Bill asked as he pulled into the gravel driveway that he was sure at one time had been concrete.

The storm door on the left half of the duplex dangled precariously, its hold on the house down to just a single bolt. Bill and Seth were reaching into their pockets for their credentials when the storm door banged loudly against the house. A man with faded blue jeans, a stretched out Arctic Monkeys t-shirt, a long ponytail and wild looking beard, stepped onto the porch. Lighting the cigarette that dangled from his lips, he asked, "You boys looking to rent one of my houses?"

The agents had neither the time, nor the patience to deal with his obvious sarcasm, and, as if they'd rehearsed the move, simultaneously flipped open their billfolds to reveal the ID's that put the FBI logo front and center.

Bill was professional, yet pointed when he asked, "are you the owner of this duplex?" Already knowing the answer, he continued, "We're with the Federal Bureau of Investigation, and want to speak with Luke Johnson. Will you get him, please?"

The landlord twirled his beard, took a long drag of the cigarette that still dangled from his mouth, and waited for the curling smoke to dissipate before he answered. "He ain't here. He ain't been here since he rented the dump. What do you want him for?"

Seth stepped forward and waved the smoke away from his face, "What do you mean he hasn't been here? Are you sure you haven't seen him? I'd hate to pull you away from all of this and arrest you for impeding an investigation. Who would make sure your tarp stayed down during a storm?"

Bill gave Seth a tone-it-down look and tried a different approach. "He's been out for six months, how is he paying his rent if he hasn't been back?"

"He ain't been by to pay no rent because he paid for six months up front, cash money when he took the place, and I'm tellin' you, I ain't seen him since."

"What about his stuff," Seth asked. "Do you mind if we look inside his unit?"

"I don't care if you go in, but the joint came furnished and he never did move any clothes, or anything else in."

Careful of where they stepped on the rotting front porch, the men put gloves on, and stepped into the house. They made their cursory search through drawers and cupboards, but quickly discerned that the landlord was telling the truth. There was nothing personal inside the unit. Bill handed the man a card before they got in the car and told him to contact him immediately if Johnson came back.

"How many cons have enough money when they get out to pay six months of rent up front?" Seth asked Bill as they sped down the side street toward the main road. Bill looked at his longtime partner and wondered, not for the first time, how many pair of Levi jeans he had, because they were always sharply creased, and were paired perfectly to his polo shirts and navy blazer.

Bill pulled his sunglasses from the visor, and replied, "They don't, which makes our next interview even more important. Sounds like this attorney, who, according to Abbey, is connected, may have some information. Give Kate a call. They're going to see Johnson's ex. Have them push her on that front as well."

"Agreed, and I also wonder how a repeat offender and habitual tenant of the prison system would be able to afford a connected attorney. I'm going to ask Abbey to follow the money," Seth replied, using finger quotes around the word "afford."

Bill turned back onto Woodward Avenue and replied, "Agreed, and ask her to dig deeper on what Johnson was in for, and why he got out."

CHAPTER 15

DAY TWO - 8:30 AM

Auburn Hills, MI

Jane exited I-75 at Baldwin Road in Auburn Hills, and was astonished at the transformation to the area. She remembered the exit when there was just a single gas station on the corner, and that a few miles east of it, just beyond where the road turned to gravel, was an ice-cream shop which had been a regular summertime destination. She smiled at the memory because she went with her next-door neighbor, who was also her babysitter and best friend's mom. Whenever Tad went out of town on what they all believed at the time to be business trips, she'd stay with them. Hindsight being what it is, Jane now realized that those were the most normal days of her childhood, and certainly the happiest.

Kate checked the GPS on her phone and directed Jane to take the first left beyond the million-acre shopping mall which was new since she left.

"Tonya Baxter is in that condo complex there on the right," Kate instructed. "Building 113, unit 2."

Before the agents could ring the doorbell, a woman who looked a decade older than the 42 trips around the sun they knew she'd made, stepped outside. Judging from the dark circles that smudged the pale skin beneath her jaundiced eyes, the pocked scarring on her face, and rotting teeth, Jane assumed it was lifestyle, not genetics that had stolen her vitality and youth.

With her badge held in front of her, Kate made the introductions: "Good morning, I'm Kate Jenkins, and this is my partner, Jane Newell. We're from the FBI. We have a few questions to ask about your ex-husband, and his former cellmate, Tad Wilkins. Could we come in for a few minutes?"

Instead of standing back to let them in, the woman stepped all the way on to the porch and closed the door behind her.

Lighting the cigarette she carried out with her, Miss Baxter said, "I was just coming out to smoke, we'll have to talk out here. I ain't seen Luke since before he got out. He set us up in this swanky joint and took off. If he's in trouble again, I know nothin' about it, but would bet my last nickel on that Wilkins fella bein a part of it."

Jane exchanged a look with Kate who nodded the go ahead for Jane to continue.

"Tad Wilkins is still in prison and is never getting out. How could he be getting Luke in trouble again? Is Luke here, now?"

Tonya lit a fresh cigarette from what was left of the first one before flicking it into the bushes.

Tonya tapped her temple and said, "Luke's kinda thick up in the noggin, fried what brain cells God did give him with too much dope when he was just a young kid, and he thinks Tad Wilkins is God or something. Honest, I think he fell in love with him, probably even started eating from the other side of the buffet, if you know what I mean."

Jane was flabbergasted at Tonya's statement but knew not to make eye contact with Kate. They'd laugh about it later, but right now, they had more questions, so she tapped her shoulders so Kate would know she was turning it back to her to continue.

Kate indicated they should all take a seat in the Adirondack chairs on the porch, and asked Tonya, "Have you seen him since he got out, and what do you mean, he set you up in this condo?"

Tonya tossed her cigarette butt into the bushes before she

answered, "No, he ain't been around, at all. In fact, it was that sleazy lawyer of his that gave me the address and the keys."

Jane's relief from breathing the second-hand smoke was brief as Tonya lit another cigarette, but she moved on with her next question.

"So, please help me understand why you went to the prison to see him even though you're divorced, and now that he's out, you haven't seen him at all. Do you know where the money came from to pay for this place?"

"I went because that lawyer dude told me if I went to see him that he'd help us get out the ghetto. I been clean and sober for nine months now, but I wouldn't be if I was still in Pontiac. And I didn't ask no questions from nobody about the money."

"Congratulations," Kate told her with a newfound respect, "I'm clean and sober going on ten years, so I know the battles you're fighting. Why do you think Luke was in love with Tad?"

"Maybe in love ain't exactly it, but there was something not right about it. It's like Luke was under a spell or something, and I know he'd a done anything the man asked of him. There was something off about Wilkins, and I'm sure he can get crap done, even from inside."

Jane and Kate nodded their agreement that they'd gotten all they would get out of her for now, so they stood up, and Kate handed Tonya a card and asked her to please call if she heard from her ex-husband. As in tune with one another as they were, they both laughed at Tonya's comment about the other side of the buffet once they were in the car.

"Does that mean what I think it means?" Kate asked, and then said, "Never mind, I don't really care. But when she talked about moving away from Pontiac, she intimated it was taken care of for more than just her. Makes me wonder if she's waiting for her ex to come home."

After directing Kate back to the expressway, Jane quietly contemplated the statement Tonya made about Tad being able to get things done, even from a maximum-security prison. Her first instinct was that it would be impossible, but she couldn't discount the reference to the name only her father ever called her in the text message she'd gotten. Is he in contact with someone on the outside, she wondered, and as she'd done several times already this morning, contemplated telling Kate about the message. Her reasoning for keeping it to herself, at least for now, hadn't changed. She still believed that the press had figured out who she was and leaked it to someone who wanted to play head games with her, and she wasn't willing to compromise her spot on the team because of a veiled, and most certainly failed attempt to make her crazy.

"You'll want to make a left off the next exit," she said to Kate, "that'll take us right into Holly, and to Allison's and Mandy's houses. Hopefully they remembered something overnight that will help."

As Kate was turning left onto East Holly Road, Jane felt her phone buzz inside her messenger bag. Unlocking her screen to what she assumed would be a team text, Jane's heart suddenly felt like it froze mid-beat when she read the ominous message about their third victim, Eve Laraby. Jane kept her head bent over her bag and tried to regulate her breathing and control the glistening blush on her face. She hadn't processed the note yet and wasn't ready to share it.

"Hey, are you ok over there?" Kate asked, "I'll take the lead on this first interview, no worries."

Jane opened the water bottle she'd pulled out of her bag and nodded her understanding. With her heartbeat under control, Jane ignored her better judgment about sharing the mysterious messages, pushed the text to the back of her mind and closed the door on it. This was her first victim interview and she wanted to be present for it.

The door opened as the agents were walking up to the door, and a woman who looked to be in her mid-fifties balanced a baby in one arm and held the storm door open with the other. Her flawless pale skin seemed to pair perfectly with her auburn red hair that was drawn back into a tight braid, and although her eyes were rimmed a fiery red, the emerald-green color of them still shone like a beacon.

With her free hand extended, she introduced herself, "Good morning, agents. We've been expecting you. I'm Shannon O'Malley, Mandy's mom, and this," she said with a kiss to the top of a fuzzy head, "is Joseph, Jr. JJ for short."

"Thank you for seeing us," Kate told her, "We are so very sorry for your loss. Is Mr. Leonard home? We just have a few questions and won't keep you too long."

Mrs. O'Malley nodded and gestured toward a visibly heartsick young man sitting on the couch. His raw, red eyes seemed to be glazed over as he stared, almost trance-like at the gallery of family photos on the wall. Jane went weak in the knees and felt a dizzying sense of vertigo at the sight of the poor young father, and had to swallow the bile that rose in her throat. She reminded herself that this was not her father's work, but it was a struggle knowing that at least 15 times, her own father had caused this type of paralyzing torment.

Jane shook her head to put her brooding reverie in check when Kate stood to leave, but instead of joining her at the door, she sat on the ottoman directly in front of the young widower.

He looked at her as she took his hands into hers, and said very quietly, "We are going to find the person that did this to Mandy, and things may get pretty crazy, but I want you to know there's a good possibility that Mandy's killer has a family who have no idea what he's doing – and if they could, they would want to apologize to you for the pain he's caused."

Joe Leonard's blank stare locked on Jane. "How do you know they'll want that?" Jane had no idea how to answer his question and was glad when Kate touched her elbow to leave.

When she stood up to leave, Jane could tell by Kate's body language that she was not happy, but wasn't sure if, like her, she felt the tremendous grief of this family, or if there was another reason.

"You're better on these rural roads, and I'd like to drive Mandy and Allison's routes, maybe find a possible abduction site."

Jane caught the keys Kate tossed and made her way out of town.

Uncomfortable with the silence, Jane looked at her mentor, and wondered if her focus out the side window was because she was looking for a good spot for a predator to hide, or if her thoughts were elsewhere.

"What's up, Kate? You're awfully quiet over there. Do you want to talk about that interview?"

Kate looked at her, and after a couple of false starts, seemed to find the words she was looking for.

"It was awful, and definitely the hardest part of our job, but my concern is mostly for you. I got the feeling when you were speaking to Mr. Leonard, that you were making it too personal, almost like you were apologizing for Tad. You cannot make this investigation personal. Your father did not murder those women."

It was Jane's turn for some silent reflection and soul searching, and Kate, knowing her as well as she did, realized that and went back to searching for breaks in foliage big enough for a vehicle to lay in wait, yet concealed enough to go unnoticed.

Kate turned back to Jane when she came out of her quiet contemplation, and said, "Right after they put my father in the squad car and I knew there was no mistake, my breath felt like syrup was crowding the air out of my chest. I remember falling to my knees and looking around for the first time since they stormed my house. My best friend and her mom were watching from their driveway. I'll never forget the look of shock in their eyes, or how their rigid jaws hung down to their chests. I haven't seen, nor spoken to them since that day."

With her focus still on the road, Jane took a deep breath and continued, "Squad cars and FBI vehicles lined my road in a display much like a dancing fountain, except the lights were the ones flashing from atop the cars, and the music was the sirens. Down the center of my street were news vans, and the neighbors stood mute in their driveways, staring at the spectacle while I tried to make sense out of what had just happened. Since that day," Jane went on, "I've wished I could apologize to the families he destroyed."

"I know," Kate said, "I remember talking you out of tracking them all down about five years after the fact."

Jane smiled then and added, "And you were right. That would've just opened their wounds all over again, but do you remember what you told me?" Without waiting for a reply, Jane continued, "You told me I could still help them, by helping to stop other monsters just like Tad Wilkins from ruining other lives."

Jane and Kate both took a moment to recall the conversation when Jane declared, "That's still my goal, and you're right, I made it too personal with Mr. Leonard. I will tattoo it on my brain if I must, but I will remember that this, and any other cases I work, will be separate cases, and not the work of Tad Wilkins."

The two ladies shared a fist bump but were interrupted by Kate's text message alert.

"It's from Abbey. The disposal site property used to be yours."

CHAPTER 16

DAY TWO - 5:00 PM

MSP Incident Center

Jane and Kate followed the smell of fresh coffee right into the incident room, where the rest of the team, including Commander Murphy and Sam were just getting settled. The two men from Michigan seemed to be having a quiet, yet heated discussion in the corner, but Jane took notice of Sanchez, standing with his arms crossed up near the front of the room. His stiff body, and tightly clenched jaw indicated that again, he was not a happy agent.

From the front of the room, Bill called the group to attention.

"I'd like to hear how everyone made out today. Hopefully we'll have a few more pieces to add to the puzzle. Kate and Jane, would you like to start?"

They decided on the way in that Jane would speak first, because she needed to explain how the dumpsite came to be in her name.

"We spoke to both husbands, and their parents, but other than their wives working hard to get their pre-pregnancy bodies back, and six-month-old babies, they had nothing in common. It's a small town, so they knew of each other, but did not run in the same social circles, attend the same church, or even go to the same exercise classes. Both men think they'd have noticed if anyone, or anything seemed out of place."

Jane took a sip of coffee and was about to continue when Sanchez interrupted, "How do you explain, agent Newell, the fact that you once owned the property where the bodies were disposed?"

Jane took a deep breath, and keeping her cool, calmly explained.

"I've never seen that property, and never even knew where it was. As it turns out, it was 200 acres with a cabin that Wilkins bought, in my mother's name. It's where he took his victims to torture and kill. Long after he was incarcerated, when I was at VCU, I received a certified letter with a deed to the property."

"So, if you saw the deed, you must've known where it was," Sanchez barked.

"No, I didn't. All I saw was a legal description and learned from the letter that since it was legally my mom's, and she was deceased, I was the legal heir to it. I did not want it, never even wanted to see it, so I contacted the State of Michigan and signed the deed over to them. I donated it, and in turn, they forgave all the back taxes on it. I later learned that the cabin had been demolished."

Seth stood up then with the account of his and Bill's day.

"That may be significant, but for now, let's move on. Luke Johnson is in the wind, but we need to find him. There is more to his story than we know, and according to Kate, they felt the same way with Tonya, his ex-wife. Sal Faraci did seem like a sleezy character, but of course hid behind client privilege and gave us nothing."

Bill stood up and added to Seth's report that Abbey was going to do an even deeper dive into him. "He seemed to have a lot more money than a convict should have when they get out, so she's going to follow that. We also need to know how he was able to get out when he hadn't even gone to trial yet, for his third offense."

Sam and Sanchez both stood up at the same time, but Sam did the talking, and Jane wondered if she was the only one who noticed Sanchez's body tense up.

"We didn't get a whole lot from Kyle Laraby, just that she either jogged, or went to aerobics class every day. Lots of times she ran with the little fella in his fancy stroller, but not always. One of the neighbors did say that he'd seen a white van in the neighborhood a couple of times, and it was moving slow, but figured he was checking out the house for sale up the block. Kyle saw it too, and said he'd seen that van one day when he was at the park with Eve and the baby. That was about a week ago."

"That was good work, guys," Seth said, and then added, "we'll have Abbey check the traffic cameras, maybe we'll get lucky."

"I sure hope so," Bill said, "Eve Laraby is running out of time, we need to get something that fits, and fast, because tomorrow is day three."

Jane felt a tremendous amount of sadness for what poor Eve was going through at that moment, and the anxiety she had about her last text message was beginning to mount again. The two messages she'd gotten had come from unknown senders, with no identifying number, and seemed to disappear after she'd read them. Fortunately, she had the forethought to screen shot them so when she did take it to Kate, she would have the exact verbiage. She was waging an internal battle with herself over whether she should or should not show them to the team. At this point she did not believe it would make a difference, but vowed to herself that if she thought, even for a minute that they'd help find Eve, she would turn them over immediately.

Acting on a hunch, Jane suggested they have Abbey get the plat maps for all the property surrounding the disposal site.

"It's all state land," Sanchez huffed, "what the hell good is it going to do? I think it's a waste of time."

Of all the people on the team, Sam is the one who responded. As if he'd been holding in his frustration for the agent all day, he said, "That ain't a bad idea. You never know what might back up to that land until you see it all. Them woods is pretty thick over there, and if any of it is privately owned, we can run backgrounds on them."

Already reaching for his phone, Seth told them, "If nothing else, it's another line to tug, and hopefully more people to talk to. I'm going to have her email it to you, Kate. Maybe you'll be able to study it tonight."

"That all sounds like a plan," Bill said, "and now I think we need to eat. Patrick recommends a place up the road with decent bar food. Why don't we go there? We can put the case on pause and enjoy a meal and a drink."

With Sanchez taking his assigned seat in the back of the Ford, and Jane at the wheel, they headed out to the Bottoms Up Bar and Grill just up Dixie Highway. Jane was grateful for the quiet drive because she was trying to process what they knew that could help them find Eve Laraby alive. As distressing as it was, she knew they didn't have enough pieces yet to complete the puzzle and could hear Kate's imaginary voice tell her that an investigation is a step-by-step process, where you gather everything, because you don't know what's going to be important – until it is.

Jane's head-space was so engrossed in trying to figure out a way to bring Eve home to her family, that she didn't realize the group had decided on pizza for all.

Kate poured a glass of ice water from the pitcher on the table, and as she started to pour one for Jane, said, "Don't worry little bird, we got one with all veggies. I know you aren't a fan of processed meats."

Jane thanked her partner and as she picked up her glass for a drink, she had an idea on where she could get some answers and a few more pieces to the puzzle.

Jane sensed it wasn't anything she could share just yet with the team, so she made a snap decision and asked Bill if she could use the SUV in the morning, and hopefully get some information that will lead them to Eve within the killer's timeline.

"I connected with an old friend and would like to have breakfast with her," she said, "but it'll be early, and I won't be too late for the morning briefing."

Bill told her he had no problem with that, "Kate and Sanchez, you can ride in with Seth and I in the morning. Just try not to be too late, Jane. The way I figure it, all we have is tomorrow to find Eve Laraby alive."

The snap decision she'd made to go to the prison in the morning seemed to hammer at her every nerve, and her suddenly dry mouth, and rapid breaths warned her of an impending panic attack as they drove back to the hotel. The attacks were almost a daily occurrence in the years following Tad's arrest, so she focused on the tools Dr. Isles gave her to thwart them. Kate's voice was also a great tool to snap her out of her out of her reverie and back to her reality.

As they walked into the lobby, Kate told Jane that the email with the plats of all the property surrounding the dumpsites came through, so she was going to stop at the business center to print them. "How about if we meet in your room after our work out and go over them?"

Jane nodded her agreement and told her she'd meet her in the fitness room. She needed a couple of minutes to contemplate the decision she'd made – while she still had time to change her mind.

With her hair still wrapped in a towel after her post workout shower, Jane disengaged the safety lock and opened the door for Kate.

"I cleared off that table so we could spread out," Jane told her, "But maybe we should use the other bed. That looks like a lot of papers."

"It is," Kate answered as she set her purse down on the coffee counter. "Let's use the bed. If we lay them out in the right positions, it might make it easier to read."

They approached the laying out of the forest the same way they would a puzzle: outside properties first, working their way to the middle. Whatever was left was where their thoughts would be focused.

"Ok, look up here, in the far NW corner of the state land, it looks like a teeny tiny corner of it butts up to this private parcel." Jane was holding a plat sheet that showed a triangular parcel of land, met right at the tip with the state land.

"Good catch, rookie," Kate said, "I'm going to text Abbey that parcel's information and have her find out who owns it. We've already determined the unsub must have a 4X4 of some sort to transport the women. This could be a good lead."

When Kate bid her goodnight and left the room, Jane's stomach lurched with the notion that she wasn't fooling her good friend about her breakfast meeting. She really hoped Kate wouldn't call her out, because if asked, Jane knew she'd never be able to lie. She figured she could tell her that her preoccupation was because she'd been thinking about Nick, and it wouldn't be a total lie. She was convinced, though, that he would not send her frightening text messages. That left only one other person privy to the blood chilling nickname, and she planned to deal with him personally. Jane thought again about coming clean with her training agent but decided to wait. If she could get information on how to find Eve, then all this subterfuge and her sour stomach and worn nerves, would be worth it.

CHAPTER 17

DAY TWO - 11:00 PM

Rural Oakland County

"Darling, Eve, we're almost done now. I'm going to give you a whiff of my magic elixir to relax you, and then I'm going to cut your zip ties off. When I'm done, you won't need them anymore."

I loved this part of my game, although Eve has been a bit disappointing. She didn't seem to have the strength to fight as hard as Mandy and Allison did. She wanted to fight, her terror-stricken eyes made that quite clear, but she lacked the physical endurance the other two had. But I intended to follow my patient, well planned ritual because I worked so hard to hone it. My practice kills were just random acts that I carried out in haste, like a petulant child throwing an angry temper tantrum. The reason for the practice kills, according to OMK, was to make sure I even had a taste for taking a life.

"Not everyone has the chops for it," he told me in one of his letters, "but I chose you because I think that you do."

I'll admit to being nervous my first time, but I was nervous before riding my first roller coaster, too. After that first ride, though, I couldn't get back in line quickly enough to do it again. Killing was like my adult roller coaster ride that I kept wanting to repeat. Watching the life go out of a woman's eyes is the most gratifying experience I'll ever have, and the very best part is knowing that I was the last person they would ever see. Finally I felt seen, and I had OMK to thank for it.

I didn't need to have sex with the women because when I'd take them to the brink of death with the rope around their throats, my orgasm when they coughed and sputtered back to life after I loosened the hold, was the best release I'd ever known.

Burning my message into the backs of the three women was impossible to do while they were hogtied, so I always saved it for the last night because by then they were too weak, and their limbs too disarticulated to move. I did dose them with my homemade ether cocktail before that part of the ritual because it knocked them out and kept them still. Burning designs into a living person's back with a glowing, red-hot fireplace poker is not as easy as it would seem.

It took less than 30 seconds from the time I put the soaked rag under Eve's nose for her to lose consciousness, so I got right to work. With the bolt cutters I kept handy, I cut through the zip ties that held her, and flipped her to her stomach. It dawned on me that this would complete my message to the FBI, at least for this round of murders, because this was not the end of my ride. The adrenaline spike I get during the abduction and torture is now as necessary to me as the air I breathe. It is an addiction, and one I have no intention of trying to break.

As I finished my work on Eve's back, I heard the shrill tone of my burner phone. Happy to be hearing from OMK, I turned the still unconscious Eve on to her left side and grabbed my phone.

Glad to know you're having the time of your life, but the process of Operation Janey is moving too slow. You need to step up that part of the game and get that wimpy Sanchez to do the same. You do NOT want to make me sorry that I chose you. Remember, the one who made you can also end you.

Damn it, the threat embedded in that text was disturbingly transparent, but I no longer need Tad's blessing and, I am not going to stop killing. I do agree that Sanchez needs to step it up, and I think I have the perfect way to burrow deep into Jane Newell's head. Having my own lackey is almost as fun as hunting humans – almost.

"I'm going to leave for a while, darling Eve," I called out to her, but when I walked back to what I refer to as the torture pit, I picked up my step when I noticed Eve's eyes, still taped open, were not darting right, and left like usual, but were fixed straight ahead, and lifeless.

"What the hell? I'm not ready yet. I still have another full day of play planned out."

How dare she die on her own. Looking into their eyes as they take their final leave is like the crowning point of my work, and to have missed that with Eve has left me feeling woefully unfulfilled. But accidents happen, so I cannot allow this situation to throw me back to the days when I felt invisible, and insignificant. There will always be more women.

"Ok, darling Eve, a change in plans," I said to the dead woman as I hoisted her over my shoulder and carried her out to the van. When I opened the sliding door and rolled her lifeless body inside, I noticed my black abduction bag and smiled at my bright future.

CHAPTER 18

DAY THREE – 5:00 AM

Quality Inn – Holly, MI

Sanchez was awakened early to the incessant vibrating of his burner phone, and while he wanted to turn it off and go back to sleep, he was curious what the day's message would be. The messages he'd gotten so far hadn't given him any clues as to exactly what information his anonymous ally had that would connect Jane to her father's crimes and ultimately tank her career.

Things are starting to move along rather quickly, and if you want to emerge the hero of your elite team, you need to do a better job getting into Jane's head. She needs to be weakened to the point of collapse when we drop the final hammer. Have you asked yourself why she hasn't taken your cryptic texts to her bosses?

Sanchez, fully awake now, walked to the window, and looked at the parking lot below while the in-room coffee pot sputtered out his first of many cups for the day. He wondered briefly who his ally was, and how they knew Jane hadn't shared the messages, but put it aside because he really didn't care. As his morning vision became acclimated to the darkness, he saw Jane getting into the SUV. Her ink black hair was piled on top of her head and not cascading in curls down her back like usual, but when she tossed the bag she was never without on to the front seat, he knew he was not mistaken.

"I don't know what that bitch is up to," he said to the empty room, "but I'm sure it's not a breakfast date. Seems to me it's a good time to say good morning."

Picking up his secret phone, he decided to start his day's conversation rather simply.

Where were you going so early this morning, Janey?

Having crafted the second message in his head, he decided he'd wait a bit before sending it, and started the shower water running.

CHAPTER 19

DAY THREE – 5:00 AM

Westbound I-96

Jane had turned her phone off and buried it at the bottom of her messenger bag before she got into the car. After waging a mental debate on the pros and cons of it, she'd made up her mind to make this visit today. She also knew without a doubt that if Kate called her, she would own up to where she was going, and Kate, being who she is, would talk her out of it.

Jane set her cruise control when she got onto I-96 and headed west towards the Ionia State Penitentiary. Once again, she considered her plan, and her goal for this visit. A part of her wished that she'd been up front with the mysterious texts from the start, even if it meant she'd be off the case. She felt confident though that she would be able to contribute to the team's success in capturing this new lunatic. The last two days had shown her, if nothing else, that she was doing what she was meant to do. Saving Eve Laraby's life is what mattered, and she had a hunch that Tad Wilkins would hold some information to help make that happen.

The truck's dashboard GPS alerted her that she'd arrived at her destination, so she pulled into the parking area reserved for law enforcement and stowed her gun in the locked weapons compartment. As she stepped out of the car and made her way to the entrance, she took a deep cleansing breath and reminded herself why she was here. Taking the fact that it was her father out of the equation, she reminded herself that she was here, as an FBI agent, to interview a psychopathic serial killer in the hopes of catching another one.

With her credentials at the ready, Jane was buzzed through the first of many reinforced, automatic doors and was met by a guard.

"I'm Jane Newell," she said with confidence, "and am here to meet with inmate 67049, Tad Wilkins." Knowing approval wasn't needed if the meeting involved an active case, she added, "It's regarding an open investigation."

"Yes ma'am," the guard replied with barely a cursory glance at her ID. "Please place your personal belongings in the locker."

As Jane was securing her messenger bag into the locker, another door opened electronically with an earsplitting clarion call. As the guard stepped through the opening, he told Jane that it would take about 15 minutes to get the prisoner secured in an interview room, and then invited her to relax until he returned.

The piercing beep started again as the door closed behind him, which left Jane essentially locked in a room barely big enough for a desk and a chair, which to her mind, was not real conducive to a relaxing wait. As she'd done hundreds of times when her mind went quiet, Jane reflected on the day he was arrested, and the years that followed. She wondered, not for the first time, if her dad's warm and loving smile had returned, or if she'd face the person incapable of empathy or love, even for his only child. She'd had enough therapy and taken enough behavioral psychology classes to know what she'd see in there, but couldn't stop her mind from wondering.

Jane tried hard to keep her mind focused on the questions she was going to ask, but her thoughts kept circling back to the first year after his capture. Her Aunt Judy, with the help of her therapist, Dr. Isles, spent countless hours guiding her through memories of her years with a killer father. They didn't want to just tell her how good he was at manipulating those around him, they wanted her to see it for herself, and more, to realize that he was such an expert with masks, that he fooled everyone.

She remembered Dr. Isles's exact words that helped kick her real recovery into gear.

"Tad Wilkins controlled and manipulated how he was viewed, and he did it as well as anyone I've ever studied. No one was going to see his true self until he was good and ready for them to see it. Not even you."

The almost deafening beep of the electronic door in front of Jane started its staccato warning again and drew her out of her mind and back to the present situation. The guard told her the inmate was ready and offered concise, almost brusque instructions.

"Follow me, agent, and look either straight ahead or at the floor, and keep your arms to your sides at all times. We will be going through a series of hallways where the doors will open ahead of us, and close behind us, but stay behind me and you'll have no trouble."

Jane focused on separating her job from her DNA with deep breaths meant to relax what felt like a tightly wound ball of nerves in the pit of her stomach. With her eyes cast downward as instructed, she noted that the many years of grime smeared into the tile floor made it impossible to determine what the original color was. The layers of security were clear with the iron gates and barriers that rose ahead of her and slammed shut behind her. The ear-piercing alarm that preceded them did little to stop her body from jolting with every thunderous clang. The shrill staccato type of beep seemed like an alert to anyone nearby that the dingy hallway was being used. A thud to her right had her instinctively turn so she was eye to eye with an inmate who had his face smashed against the shatter proof window on the cell's door.

After another set of opening and closing gates, the guard stopped and turned his head toward a reinforced door with what he explained was a one-way window into the interview room. She could see in, but the occupant could not see out. Jane hesitated long enough to fill her lungs with a slow intake of air, and then stepped up to the window for the first sighting of her father in thirteen years. His hair, while still dense and cropped short, no longer looked like perfectly painted on black shoe polish. The lustrous shine he'd once been so proud of now seemed dull and faded, peppered with enough gray to make it appear dingy. He was tethered by chains to a faded green table and a heavy oak chair that were cemented into the floor. His ankles were also shackled and secured to cemented-in floor rings.

With a computerized key card, the guard reached around Jane to open the door.

As if he sensed this was her first prison visit, the guard's voice was soft when he said, "He can't hurt you agent, but there's a button on the wall just inside the door. When you're ready, just push it and I'll let you out."

Jane nodded her understanding, but just before she stepped into the room, wondered how he could be staring right through her if he could not see out the window. She noted that his eyes looked as empty and dark as the last time she'd seen him, but now held an almost knowing gleam, like he had a secret he couldn't wait to share. Without the benefit of his bi-annual teeth bleaching, the crooked, diabolical grin he flashed at her had yellowed quite considerably. When Jane stared into his cold eyes, she knew that the soulless man before her was nothing more than a sperm donor. Intellectually she'd always known it, but the epiphany she just had on an emotional level had her feeling as if she'd shed a heavy coat of armor.

Her legs felt like stone as she moved slowly into the room, and she hoped he couldn't see the thumping rhythm of her throat pulse as she sat in the chair facing him, because she knew he'd get off on what he would perceive as weakness. She needed to keep the upper hand if she was going to bring any helpful information back to her team.

"Well hello, Janey. I've been waiting for you." His raspy voice, and the way his adam's apple rippled in the column of his wrinkled throat when he used that nickname, sent tight coils through her stomach, but she never broke eye contact when she inhaled a steadying breath and replied.

"It's just Agent. I haven't been Janey in thirteen years, but I am curious as to whom you may have shared that nickname with. After all, you always said it was your special name for me."

"Oh, I know exactly who and what you are, *Agent Newell,* and I know why you're here. One of my admirers has picked up where I left off, and you want my help." Jane's eyes slammed into his with a fiery glare and a fierce mask she hoped would conceal her inner turmoil as her racing mind tried to make sense of his statement, when he continued, "But first, a family reunion. I heard Aunt Judy is finally shacking up with her girlfriend. How does that make you feel, *Janey*?"

Jane was instantly stunned silent because this interview was not going as she'd envisioned it would. She expected to be in control of it, powerful enough in her position to prove, that in spite of him, she was a bad ass woman, but instead, her brain wouldn't clear out enough to formulate an intelligent sentence. She considered her training, and oddly enough found herself smiling when she heard Kate's voice instead of her instructor's. What in the hell were you thinking of coming in here without telling the team? You aren't ready for this. Hell, even the most experienced interviewers struggle with psychopaths.

As it always did, Kate's imaginary voice grounded her enough to lean in, and with the palms of her hands planted firmly on the nasty desk, delivered an expressive reply.

"There will never be a reunion. I came to ask if you'd shared your sick leanings with any of your, as you so aptly stated, admirers, or if you have any inside knowledge of a copycat."

The inmate's throat resonated with a low mocking chuckle, and Jane cringed when he leaned forward and said, in an eerie, sinister sounding voice, "Now, now, Janey, you know you can't take without giving. Tell me more about Kate and the team, your new apartment, and hell, even your cat. I get so little stimulating conversation in here."

Jane stood sharply and turned her back on the man she called dad for fifteen years. She was at once shocked by his knowledge of her life, the fact was that she was not going to get anything useful out of him, and most frightening of all, she wondered if he was a threat to Kate and her team. She'd wanted to ask him about Luke Johnson, but her muddled mind wouldn't allow her to turn back and face him.

Jane pressed the button to call for the guard, and as the door opened, Tad told her, "We will be talking again, Janey, you can count on it, and oh by the way, do you plan on telling Kate that we chatted today?"

Even with her back to him, Jane could sense the smirk on his face, and was determined to have the final word, so as she stepped out of the room, she said, "By the way, the person copying your kills is better at it than you ever were."

By the time Jane heard the door slam shut, she and the guard were already on their way back through the labyrinth of hallways with the ear-piercing blare of alarms as the gates opened and shut seemingly on their own. She was so focused on the not so veiled inferences her father made about her life, that she didn't realize she was back where she started until the guard spoke.

"Okay, agent, once you gather your belongings from the locker, I'll let you out."

Muscle memory kicked in when she thanked him and retrieved her bag. The bright morning sun, as she stepped outside, had her digging into her bag for sunglasses. The sun had just begun to break dawn when she arrived, so she was seeing the decrepit, concrete structure for the first time. The massive complex was surrounded by 12-foot wire barriers connected to massive steel beams and topped with razor wire and a stun fence. Cloud reaching gun towers that reminded her of a rook on a chess board made her feel as if her every move was being followed by a sniper rifle. It was a bleak and brooding sight against the blazing fall sunshine, so she drew in a lungful of fresh air, and settled in for her drive back to the State Police Post, in Holly.

She was ahead of schedule and was relieved to realize she could stop for a cup of coffee for the road and would still get back in time for the morning briefing. Coffee always seemed to help her think things through and she needed some clarity. She had no illusions that Wilkins was only intimating his knowledge of her life, of Aunt Judy's life, and of her team. He even knew she had a new apartment and a cat, so her thoughts had to be in the form of a threat assessment of what he could, or could not, accomplish from his maximum-security prison cell. Adding to that line of thought, she also had to weigh the significance of the text messages she'd gotten, and whether or not he could be behind those as well.

"I think the choice is out of my hands now," she said aloud to an empty car, "I must tell Kate. Hopefully once she calms down, she'll be able to help me figure out this mess I seem to have walked into."

Jane spotted a Speedway gas station at the next exit and pulled off to use the facilities and get some coffee. When she pulled into the parking space, she remembered her phone was still at the bottom of her bag, so she dug it out, and turned it on. She expected to see a missed call or two from Kate, but instead she was alerted to missed text messages. She forgot about her coffee or the call of nature when she read the two missed notes:

Where were you going so early, Janey?

And the second one, even more disturbing, read,

Your secrets must be damning if they're keeping you from sharing our communications with your team.

CHAPTER 20

DAY 3 - 8:00 AM

MSP - Incident Center

Jane set her bag down on the table and was greeted with a side stare from Kate when she took the seat beside her. She was grateful that Bill had gotten started on the briefing, because it gave her an excuse to postpone the painful conversation she needed to have with Kate.

"Good morning, everyone. Glad to see you made it back in time, Jane."

Jane forced a smile and nodded to the group, and then realized it was crucial to the case that she clear her mind and be totally present for this briefing. She didn't need the prompt, but when Bill continued, he brought it to the forefront of everyone when he reminded them that they had, at most, eight hours to find Eve Laraby alive.

"I sent the case file to a profiler at the Behavior Analysis Unit at Quantico. There aren't too many surprises in it, but I've printed it out for everyone to review."

Jane felt goosebumps on her arms when she looked down at a heavy stock, brown cardboard folder. Seeing the acronym, FBI-BAU emblazoned in black across the front was a stark reminder that she was indeed a member of an elite team, and she did what Bill was afraid she'd do – she went rogue, which put her position in jeopardy.

Bill continued with some highlights of the report, which halted her brooding thoughts.

"Our unsub exhibits both controlled, and un-controlled characteristics, and for that reason, they believe he hasn't been killing for too long, at least not with the ritual he's exhibited with our last two victims. He loves the hunt, but don't be surprised to see his methodology, and his rituals evolve, and change as he grows into his new killer persona."

Seth opened his folder, and continued, "He's estimated to be a white man between the ages 40 and 55, and if not retired, then in a job flexible enough to allow him to first stalk, and then hold and torture for three days. They believe he is financially solvent, intelligent, and must own, or have access to someplace secluded enough to transport and torture them without being seen."Bill stepped up and concluded, "This is a man who either studied the Original Mother Killer or was possibly even trained by him." Jane refused to return Sanchez's hard stare at that comment and remained focused on Bill's conclusion.

"But he's also a man who loves what he's doing and is not afraid to go off script. He's waited his whole life to find something that will make him feel significant, and he will not stop until we stop him."

"So, let's get ahead of this asshat," Seth muttered through his clenched jaw, "and stop him before he gets too comfortable."

"We need someone to check traffic cameras in and around the village, and…" Bill's daily assignments were thwarted with a swoosh of air as the room's door banged open, and a deputy burst in.

"A woman's body was just found in a ditch off Fish Lake Road, north of Grange Hall. Her eyes have been taped open, and she matches the description of Eve Laraby."

"Son of a bitch," the Commander pummeled his flat hand on the table and then bellowed. "He didn't even give us the full day. Seth was right, we have to get ahead of this asshat, and fast."

Bill grabbed his jacket off the back of the chair, and said, "Let's roll team. Something changed to break his routine. Hopefully in his rush he got sloppy and left something behind at the scene."

Seth put the file in his briefcase and added, "He's escalating, and probably hunting again. Let's get him before he gets to her."

"Stacy, call the M.E., and the crime scene unit, have them meet us there," Patrick ordered as he rushed out of the room with the rest of the group, and then as an afterthought added, "Radio quiet on this until we have an ID. I don't want Mr. Laraby to see it on the morning news."

Jane was thankful for the silent ride to the scene, and to whom they all assumed was Eve Laraby. Her mind was going in so many directions, she didn't know if she should focus on how she more than likely tanked the career she loved, or the immense grief she felt for the Laraby family. Of course, the two were intermingled because it was glaringly obvious that her impulsive choice to go to the prison did nothing to help save the poor woman who was more than likely dead before she ever got there. The speech she'd mentally prepared to give Kate seemed worthless now, too. Partly because she realized that the rationale she'd prepared as part of her argument, was just that – rationalization. For the first time since they left the airport, she was glad Sanchez was in the back seat because for now at least, she could hold on to her confession, and God help her, her career.

Jane swallowed back the stomach acid in her throat and covered her red rimmed eyes with sunglasses as they pulled off the road. Get it together, she thought. For right now at least, you are still an agent and need to speak for Eve, Mandy, and Allison, so clear your head, and find the monster responsible.

When Jane spotted the van with the acronym for Crime Scene Response Unit, CSRU, and the hearse-like station wagon conspicuously marked with the Oakland County Medical Examiner's emblem, she felt back in control of her emotions. Sam was busy closing off access to the road to ward off curious onlookers and give them room to work. When the team approached Maura, she was hunched over the deceased. They all nodded at her assistant, Stan, who took a step back to allow them to get a little closer.

Jane watched as Seth and Kate squatted down beside the woman and wondered if there was any significance to the fact that her body was lying on the shoulder of the road, and not left in the woods like the others. She knew Seth had a reputation for his almost sixth sense when it came to reading a crime scene, and that his ability to spot even the smallest of details was one of the things that made Bill's unit so successful. Jane stuffed her hands into her jacket pocket and once again chided herself for risking the opportunity she was given to be a part of, and to learn from the best.

"Something happened with this kill," Seth said as he looked away from the victim and studied the immediate surroundings, "That caused the killer to leave her in such a visible location. It almost looks like he stopped what we presume is his van, slid open the side door and just rolled her out." With that said, Jane and the rest of the team watched as Seth counted off three paces, and then looked down at the gravel in the road.

They all noticed the tread marks in the damp gravel and deduced that they could be an important lead.

"Will you have CSRU take an imprint of those tracks?" Bill hadn't even finished the question when Patrick walked over to the techs and pointed at the gravel, and then added, "He changed his routine for a reason, and if we can figure that out, we'll be much closer to stopping him."

Jane watched as Kate stepped back to the body and looked reverently down at her.

"We're going to find out what happened to you, sweet girl, we just need your help." Kate spoke softly to the young woman, "Did you make him angrier than the others and that caused him to act out a day sooner? You're going to be in great hands with Maura, she will find the answers you hold."

As Jane watched the quiet interlude between Kate and the deceased woman, she made another possibly life altering choice. If this was to be her last case with the FBI, then she was going to see it through. Her mission to cage monsters was stronger than ever, and she vowed that no matter where her choices led, or where she ended up, she would speak for the victims, and hunt down every single one she could. Her silent pledge was interrupted when she saw a slight glimmer shine out from the blood encrusted tangles in her hair.

Jane pointed it out to Maura, who squatted down and carefully untangled it.

"It looks like a locket," Jane said, "can you open it? There may be a picture inside."

"Yes, of course I can," Maura replied, and with the entire team circled around, she silently opened the heart shaped locket on the end of a dainty, gold chain to a picture of a happy couple smiling down at their newborn child.

"Rest easy Eve, you are one of theirs now," Maura said, and looked up to the circle of agents. "They're the best there is, and they will get answers for your family. In the meantime, I will take good care of you." Looking up at Stan, Maura seemed to get back into her professional persona and asked him to help get Eve into the bag.

"Kate, I'll call you as soon as I know something, but based on the stage of rigor mortis she's in, I can estimate that she's been dead less than 24 hours."

Her words and actions seemed to bring the group out of their silent musings, and back to the work at hand.

"I think it's safe to assume, by the treads and where she lay," Bill told them, "that he was traveling south on Fish Lake Road, heading toward Grange Hall. Kate and Jane, you head back north and look for a side road, or even a two track where he could have accessed this street."

Jane and Kate headed toward their rental when Patrick added that he'd send Sam over to the Laraby's home once he was finished closing off the road.

"Why don't you take Sanchez with you," Seth told the sheriff, who was very quick to reply that he would go alone and didn't need any help.

In a hushed tone, Kate turned to Jane and said, "Sounds like Sam has an issue with agent Sanchez."

Jane shrugged the remark off with a quiet laugh but wondered why everyone else didn't have issues with the arrogant man. Alone with Kate for the first time since her prison visit and resolution to share it, Jane revisited her decision – again. She knew it was the right thing to do, certainly what protocol would dictate, but her heart, and gut instincts had her holding back. She had made a vow to the three women from this case, and to all victims of horrific violence, and decided that for now, she was going to listen to the voice in the back of her head telling her to stay the course, and let the pieces fall where they may.

Chapter 21

Day Three – 9:00 AM

Ionia State Penitentiary

Well, I think my Janey is a little more like her old man that she'd care to admit. If I were capable of the emotion, I might even say I was proud of how she stood up to me. I didn't like it, and certainty cannot allow that kind of insubordination, but I do admire her moxie.

When Jane shot up from her chair and turned her back on me, I knew it was clear to her that even from behind bars I had the knowledge, and the ability to penetrate any aspect of her life that I chose. I also credit myself with the fact that she's intelligent enough to recognize the veiled threats embedded in my inferences. I must say though, that her fortitude to bounce back with the last word left me slightly perplexed – and then angry that she was able to befuddle me. Damn, she would have made a fine killing partner.

My protégé, I'm sorry to admit, is not living up to my expectation. Except for adding his own signature, he is killing as I instructed, but doesn't seem to have the mental pull with Sanchez I'd hoped. It's hard to admit, but I may be partially to blame for that. I may have built up the adventure of the hunt and the kill a little more than I should have. He was bound to find the pleasure in that on his own, and probably didn't need the extra motivation from me. No, I should have been clearer about my greatest desire, which was to infiltrate and infect agent Newell's mind. What neither of those fools know though, is that I have eyes and ears everywhere, and am made aware of what they're doing, or not doing, in as close to real time as possible. I also have contact information on all my players, so it may be time to turn the heat up just a bit.

I think it's time to change the trajectory of my plan. It's time I make another visit to the library. "GUARD."

CHAPTER 22

DAY THREE - 9:30AM

Fish Lake Road - Holly, MI

Adrian Sanchez could not believe he was tasked with going door to door and asking the residents if they had, by chance, seen a white van stop and roll a dead woman out. Of course, he didn't use that verbiage, but felt it would have been a better use of his time to contact the county road commission for footage from the traffic cameras. And when he suggested he do that, Bill said he already had Abbey on it, and he needed him in the field, but to ask the homeowners if they had any outside cameras.

There were at least a half a dozen troopers and county officers at the scene, and he was angry that he was the one who had to get his feet muddy. At least they had those vile looking combat type boots that laced up to their knees. He was wearing his Italian leather Oxfords, and they were not meant for all terrain wear. And Jane of course was assigned the cushy job of driving the roads looking for access points. Sanchez was beginning to believe that not only was Jane the favorite, but that Bill was going out of his way to give the crap assignments to him.

I'm going to have to push my co-conspirator to get me the information that'll help destroy her career, Sanchez thought, before she manipulates Bill any further. He was becoming concerned that Jane would turn Bill even more against him than she'd already done.

When Sanchez felt the vibration coming from his right pants pocket, he knew it was the burner, and was relieved that no one answered the door he'd been knocking at. He looked left and right to confirm he was alone and opened the phone. Maybe I'll get the information today, he thought, but was intrigued with the message because it included an email address he recognized from his research into Jane's life.

I'm disappointed that neither of you have been forward thinking enough to push the new agent over the ledge yet. If you want to end her as badly as I think you do, then I suggest you use this email address to hit her Achilles heel, the place she's most vulnerable. Perhaps you should ask her who she spent the morning with?

Sanchez snapped the phone shut and started down the pathway to meet Bill and Seth. He was aware of the insinuation that he send Jane's aunt an email, but needed time to craft the words. He also wanted time to process all the implications of the text. He had assumed from an earlier message that someone was working with his contact, but he believed it was just an informant and didn't give it too much thought. This message was clearly sent to someone else besides himself, from a third party, and it hinted at the possibility that maybe he was the one in control. That idea made him ill at ease because he had no intention of becoming a pawn in someone else's game, but this was about him derailing Jane Newell's career, and he would accept the assistance from wherever it came. He also knew that he was smarter, more proficient with the web, and the dark web, than anyone else, and if it ever became the prudent thing to do, he could find and then confront his ally.

For now, though, it was time to be the compliant FBI agent and join his boss and his boss's side kick in the truck to continue the investigation.

CHAPTER 23

DAY THREE - 9:30 AM

Rural back roads – Holly, MI

Jane was able to navigate the gravel roads, dodge potholes, and look out the driver's side window for a possible entry from the thick woods without veering off course. Their total concentration also helped the mental debate she was waging on whether to tell Kate about her ill-fated prison visit or not. So far, the 'or not' was in the lead.

"You really are a country girl, aren't you?" Kate asked. "I'm over here holding on to the oh-shit rod, and you're just bumping along as if it's nothing."

Jane laughed and recalled how she and her best friend used to fly down these roads on their four-wheelers.

"We used to ride these trails all the time and the warm, fall days were the best because there were no mosquitoes. During what I refer to as the connecting-the-dots part of my therapy, I realized that when Tad bought me a 4X4 without my even asking, it was just part of his act to look like the perfect single father."

Jane turned left on to nothing more than a two-track opening, and after centering the truck in the worn ruts, continued, "He frequently brought me random gifts I hadn't asked for, so when I brought a puppy home, I figured he would let me keep it, but he got really angry; like irrationally angry."

"Did he lose his temper often?" Kate asked.

"No, never. In fact, showing anger was more of an anomaly in my house, which is why his reaction was so scary. He ripped the puppy right out of my arms and left in the car with her in his arms and I never saw her again."

Kate looked quietly over at Jane and said nothing because she knew that in the years since Tad's arrest, she'd learned a lot about how a psychopath's mind works.

"It wasn't until therapy, and I remembered that for a while many pets in the neighborhood were turning up dead, that I figured out the sonofabitch probably killed her."

"Cruelty to animals, as you know, is definitely a hallmark trait of a twisted mind."

"Years later," Jane said, "the experts deemed that since he was only killing two women a year by that time, the animals were a way to keep him somewhat satisfied between kills." Jane could almost hear Kate cursing Tad Wilkins, when their quiet was interrupted by Kate's buzzing phone.

"That was Maura," she said after she read the message. "She has something we need to see at the morgue. I'm going to call Bill while you figure out how to turn this truck around."

Jane saw a small clearing ahead and put the Expedition in four-wheel drive before she turned into it and executed a three-point turn to get them headed back in the direction they came from.

Jane braced herself for the disinfectant infused smell of death before she entered the Medical Examiner's office and hoped that she would have a career long enough to be completely unaffected by it. Maura was waiting for them at the reception desk.

"Thanks for getting here so quickly," she said. "I have some interesting findings."

The women followed Maura through the front office to the same changing room they were in only two days before. Once they'd donned their white, paper-like jumpsuits, they entered the autopsy suite where the stainless steel, refrigerated storage drawers that captured Jane's attention on her first trip here, seemed like nothing more than just a backdrop now. The focal point of the room this time, was Eve Laraby on a mobile gurney in the center of the room. The dried and caked blood around her neck and in her hair had been washed away by the lab technicians since she'd been transported, but to Jane's eye, the young woman's eyes still looked pained.

Maura pulled back the white sheet that rested just below Eve's chin, and both Jane and Kate inhaled sharply when they saw the Y incision from the autopsy.

With her surgical pointer, Maura pointed to the crusted lesions around her neck.

"The first thing I noticed was that there was not as much trauma on her neck as there was on Allison and Mandy, nor did she show any petechial hemorrhaging, which is a characteristic, but not necessarily a diagnostic method to determine death by strangulation."

"So, what are you saying, that she wasn't strangled?" Kate asked.

Jane was curious as well, and added, "the marks on her neck sure look like she was strangled."

"Oh, she was strangled," Maura answered, "it just isn't what killed her. My visual examination and the X rays confirmed that her hyoid bone, which is a small, horseshoe shaped bone at the base of her neck was still intact. If she'd been strangled to death, that would be broken."

As much as she liked and respected Maura, Jane was getting impatient, and wanted her to get to the point just a little quicker, but Kate spoke before she had a chance.

"I don't mean to sound impatient, but we're racing against time. If the rope around her neck did not kill her, then what did?"

"Eve Laraby's official cause of death is cardiac arrest caused by respiratory failure. Your killer either gave her too much of his homemade ether, or the horrific pain, and multiple bouts of unconsciousness caused it. My theory is that it was a combination of them all."

"So, will you still rule it a homicide?" Jane asked, "when we catch this bastard, I want him to pay for every one of them."

"Yes, my official ruling will be cardiac arrest brought on by repeated physical and chemical torture. The full autopsy revealed a very healthy young woman with no pre-existing issues. She was much smaller than the other two, and I'd bet that your killer did not know enough to adjust his doses, or the amount of time he allowed her to go without oxygen before he loosened his choke hold."

Jane noticed that Kate had her chin tucked into her chest with the same reverent head bow that she had, but after a short moment of silence, they straightened up and got back to work.

Maura gestured to Kate that she needed a hand to roll Eve over, and said, "I'm not sure what this all means, but he burned Eve, too." She picked up her surgical pointer and showed the agents the crude markings, "If you remember, Allison had three rough looking circles, and your second victim, Mandy had those same markings, but below it there were two additional dots."

"We remember," Jane said as she opened her phone to the photos she'd taken, "and Eve has all of that, plus a third row of markings that look like two dashes and one round dot."

"We have to get those photos back to the team. We figure out if it's a message to us, and if so, what it says, then we're a heck of a lot closer to catching this monster," Kate said, and as they headed back to the changing room, thanked the doctor again for her excellent work.

"Eve Laraby had been dead no more than 12 hours when she was found. I'll add that to the report and get it over to Patrick. And ladies, it's been great working with you, and I hope you don't take it personally when I say that I hope I don't see you again for a very long time."

Jane was contemplative as they walked out to the car and asked Kate to drive back to the post. "I have an idea and need to Google a few things."

When they got back into their vehicle, Jane dug through her messenger bag until she found a notebook and a pen. When Kate asked her what she was doing, and what her idea was, she just held up a finger, shook her head and indicated that she needed a minute.

The first thing Jane did, was draw out the markings from the photos she had. Once that was done, she did an internet search for a chart that displayed the Morse Code. When Maura said one of the markings looked like a dash, and referenced dots, it's what came into her mind. The next step was to match up the crude hieroglyphics burned into their backs, with the symbols on the chart.

"Holy shit," she proclaimed after she'd deciphered the markings, "I think it's Morse Code." Jane held the notebook drawing up so Kate could see it.

"I'm driving and can't see what you're showing me, so for now, please just explain."

Jane told her how she'd connected the possibility that the killer was sending a message, to the dots and dashes of the Morse Code, and went from there. Once she determined that his crude drawings actually were dots and dashes, she was able to match the symbols to the letters they represented.

"That could be a huge find, and it fits the profile of a man who has felt invisible his whole life. I'm proud of you, Jane. Once we get back to headquarters, we'll have Patrick look at it. He's retired military and will be able to confirm what you found."

Jane felt at once validated, and deceitful. Kate's approval meant everything to her, which made her decision to withhold her visit with Tad even more painful, especially because it would seem that someone else knows about it. Her mysterious text messages were clearly coming from a third party, so she did not believe her father was the sender – but if not him, she wondered, then who?

Not only was her choice to stay on the case duplicitous, and most likely career ending, it was a trust breaker, and letting Kate down was an unintended consequence she had a hard time dealing with. In one capacity or another, Jane knew that she'd spend her life hunting down monsters but losing the best friend she'd ever had was soul crushing. Undoing it all now was not an option because the damage was already done, so her plan to stay the course and see it through, right or wrong, was the only choice she had.

CHAPTER 24

DAY THREE - 2:00 PM

Incident room – MSP

The brown paper bags that contained lunch for the team, while folded and sealed at the top, did little to contain the fragrant mixture of spicy taco seasonings and grilled onions. When Jane called from the road and offered to grab the meal and bring it back for a working lunch, everyone seemed grateful. They had a lot of information to share and brainstorming to do if they had any hopes of catching the killer before there was a fourth victim.

Jane was thankful when Patrick met them at the car to help carry in all the bags. Navigating around the potholes with everyone's lunch seemed a little risky – especially, Jane thought, for Kate in those high heels.

"Kate told me about your Morse Code theory," Patrick said to Jane, "that was good work. I'll look at the pictures when we get in."

Jane smiled and put her bags down on the table inside the door of their command center. The group descended on it like vultures, and within minutes had the bags plucked clean except for the lone spinach wrap that was Jane's. For a minute, the only sound in the room was the crinkling noise of the paper sandwich wrapping being balled up and discarded.

Bill broke the silence, "Abs has a lot of information for us, so I told her we'd call her when we were through with our updates on this end."

Kate was the first to address the group, "Sanchez, are you able to hook the camera from Jane's phone to the projection screen?"

Jane looked down, and busied herself with re-wrapping her sandwich because she was afraid her facial expression would reveal the panic she felt at turning her phone over to Sanchez. For an instant she feared that her secret text messages might be revealed, but then remembered how they all seemed to disappear moments after she read them, so she dug to the bottom of her bag and walked the phone over to him. The gleam in Sanchez's steely eyes when she passed the phone to him felt to Jane like he was telegraphing a message, or a warning to her. Instinct dictated she lower her eyes until she was clear of him, but her gut told her that he'd take it as a sign of his own superiority, so she looked squarely into his gray eyes, smiled, and thanked him for his help. Grateful for that small victory, Jane returned to her seat.

While Sanchez was hooking up the cables to project the images, Kate told the team that Eve Laraby did not die by strangulation, and explained what Maura told them about her heart failure, and what could have caused it.

"I guess that explains why the killer just rolled her out of his van on the side of the road," Seth commented, "he is probably pissed that she died before he was able to complete his ritual."

Everyone at the table nodded and chatted their agreement with Seth's assessment. Sam stood up and asked, "So, how does all that change things moving forward?"

Seth's reply was halted when Sanchez announced they were ready, and Jane walked to the front of the room with her notebook and a pen.

For those in the room who had not seen the blistering abrasions on the women's backs, an audible gasp could be heard as the horrid photo array was magnified on to the big screen. Most people go their whole lives without being witness to the atrocity of inhumanity they were looking at, and a quiet reverence filled the room as Jane explained how she determined her Morse Code theory.

"These victim pictures are in order, from the upper left. With each woman, note that an additional line of burns is present." With her pen as a pointer, Jane continued, "the markings are crude, but on Allison it looks like three circles, or dots, and on Mandy those same three are present, but also a second line with two additional circles. And finally, Eve has a third line that includes two straight lines, or dashes, and one dot." While the group was studying the gruesome images, Jane tore a page from her notebook and asked Sanchez if he could scan it on to the big screen.

"When we got back into the car it clicked that maybe they weren't just circles and lines, but dots and dashes, so as you'll see, I drew them on the paper, and then using the key I found on the internet, wrote it out."

Kate stepped up beside Jane, and went on, "As you're all aware, Patrick is retired military, and has confirmed that the crude markings on the women's backs, have spelled out SEE ME."

As if they all had a sudden need to clear their heads, the group headed out the door toward the coffee pot. The veteran agents understood that the locals needed to process what they'd seen, but were also hyper aware that their timeline between kills had just been escalated, so their hunt needed to escalate as well.

Jane watched as her team and the local law enforcement officers headed back to the conference room. She was grateful they'd be actively working again because the quiet moments were anything but quiet in her mind, as her thoughts pinballed from being thankful to be a part of this team, to admonishing herself for the hole she seemed to dig herself into. Maybe Aunt Judy will have some suggestions, she thought, on how I might be able to save my dream career, and my best friend.

Bill called the meeting back to order, "I realize those ghoulish images have probably burned themselves into your soul, but the only way to honor those women, is to find the person responsible. Seth and Kate both have a lot of knowledge into a serial killer's mind, so I'm going to let them explain where we're at with all of this."

Seth began by explaining that the macabre messages in the backs of the victims, along with their taped eyes, give credibility to their profile that this unsub is a man who has felt invisible all his life. "By torturing and killing the way he has, he feels that it will no longer be possible for anyone to ignore him."

"So, does he want to be caught?" Sam asked, "and if his message is SEE ME, is he done?"

"No, he doesn't want to be caught, just wants us to know he's out there," Kate answered, "and he is a long way from being done. This killer will not stop until we stop him. In fact, in his mind he's just getting started."

Jane noticed the concentration on the faces of everyone in attendance, except for Sanchez who seemed almost bored with the whole thing. Painfully aware that this could be the last opportunity she had to witness one of these deep examinations into the criminal mind, Jane took copious notes.

Seth resumed Kate's path, "We believe this killer got started later in life than most serials and wants to make up for lost time. And while most serial killers are very smart from a forensic standpoint because they leave little or nothing behind, a stupid mistake is what usually gets them caught."

"This unsub made a mistake with Eve, we just have to ferret it out," Kate announced. "Once we do, we'll have a much clearer path to him."

Sam, who seemed to be completely engaged, asked, "What mistakes are those? You mean like dumping the body at the side of a well-traveled road?"

"That's a great question, Sam," Kate answered, "because the answer will help us all. Dumping her how he did was a mistake, but the reason he went off like he did is because of how Eve interrupted his ritual, ruined his game so to speak." Kate gestured to Seth to continue.

"As we said in our earlier profile, this is a killer who is just getting started. We believe that he worships Tad Wilkins, and was maybe even trained by him, but this unsub is starting to go off that script to find his own way. I can't stress enough how much this killer loves what he's doing, so when Eve died a day early, and not by his hand, he felt like he'd been cheated out of an entire day." Seth gave the room a minute to digest that information.

"The M.E. said that she was probably given too much of the ether he's using and was probably left unconscious longer than she should've been. Our killer didn't know enough to adjust for Eve's smaller stature, and that was his downfall. His inexperience led to that error, so when he couldn't be the one to squeeze the life out of her, he had what could only be compared to a serial killer's temper tantrum, and just tossed her out of his van."

Jane used the lull to catch up with her notes, and to look around the room again. Getting inside the head of a sadistic killer took an emotional toll, and it was clear by the complete lack of expression on the faces of the locals, that they were relieved it wasn't a part of their normal job routine.

"In conclusion," Kate stated, "we're afraid that this killer is going to escalate, and that his judgment is going to be overcome with his need to kill, although at that point, they usually become quite reckless and are easier to catch, but we'd like to stop him before that happens."

Bill stepped up and thanked Kate and Seth for their explanations, and then signaled to Sanchez that he was ready to bring in Abbey.

"We're going to hear from Abbey now, but if anyone has any questions on the profile for Kate or Seth, check with them after the meeting."

Everyone's attention turned toward the ringing computer, as Abbey popped on screen.

"Hello, my peace fighting soldiers. Fear not, my feelings are not hurt at your lack of contact today. I know you've been warriors on the hunt for the bad guy. I have loads and loads of information for you, though."

Jane looked around and thought it was impossible not to smile at the delightful cadence Abbey's words took when she spoke, but also had to take a memory trip because she was sure that just two days ago Abbey's hair was charcoal black, piped with purple, but now it was a platinum blonde color, piped with a hot pink.

"Okay, I'll start with the information I found on the private land that butted up against the disposal ground. It is a pie shaped parcel of 160 acres and is deeded to someone who has been dead for over 10 years. But fear not my lovelies, I will track it back to the land of dinosaurs if I must, but I will find the current owner."

"Do you think you could get a satellite view of the property?" Jane asked, "it may show if there are any buildings on it because that are obviously not accounted for on the deed."

"Of course, even if I have to manipulate the satellite myself. Oops, did I say that out loud? I just meant that I'm sure I can get you some images of it."

"Someone must be keeping the taxes up to date," Bill said. "That will be a good find, Abs; keep us posted. What have you been able to find out on Luke Johnson?"

"Oh, on the elusive Mr. Johnson, I have heaps of information," Abbey told them. "I'll start with the money, which sends off all the bells because he seems to have an endless supply of it, and shouldn't because, well, he spends most of his time in prison, and they don't pay very well." Abbey paused briefly for a drink of her foam topped beverage and continued, "So far, what I've found is that the distributions are all coming from an offshore, numbered account that is cloaked in multiple shell corporations."

"Anything else stand out on the money, Abs?" Bill asked. "Can you tell how it's getting into his hands?"

"Only that the charges for his rent, and for the condo in Auburn Hills are done via electronic transfers from the connected attorney,

Sal Faraci. Another six months was just applied, by the way. But fear not, my comrades, I will find the source of that cash. I know it doesn't just appear like fairy dust in Faraci's account. It'll take a lot of back hacking and tracking, but I'll find it. I am currently running a deep search on debit cards, both foreign and at home."

"Well, it makes sense that he'd need access to cash on hand," Kate said, "and if you find it, we could trace its use, which may help us nail him down."

"What else have you unearthed on him?" Bill asked. "Did anything pop on his early release from prison?"

"Pop would be putting it mildly. Information on that whole situation burst like a firework. It was his third offense, no bond granted, and he was looking at 10-20 years for armed robbery; however, his sleaze bag lawyer got him released because, and buckle up friends, this is a biggie, the only witness to the crime was killed in an auto accident days before the trial. Coincidence? I think not."

"That does seem a little suspect," Jane said.

"I'm sending the police report, but I'll give you the cliff notes. The witness's car went careening off the 6th Street Bridge, in Grand Rapids, to the bottom of the Grand River in March of 2010. From the traffic cameras he got on the bridge at about 3:00AM, and traveling at a high rate of speed went through the guard rail and plummeted about 234 feet."

Kate looked at the report on her phone, and said, "It says there were no skid marks. I wonder why he didn't try to stop."

Patrick turned toward Sam and said, "The officer that signed off on the accident is listed on this report. Why don't you go in my office and give him a call. Maybe he'll remember something."

Jane was hopeful the responding officer would have some insight because she felt sure there was more to this than what was on the police report. What was he doing on that bridge at the least crowded time of day, she wondered, and why didn't he try to stop the car?

Abbey twirled her pencil between her fingers and continued: "Now, on the ex-wife, Tonya, well, she's had a tough go of it, but seems to be on a better road now. She actually gave birth to a baby boy about a year ago."

Jane and Kate quickly turned their heads toward each other when a small piece of the puzzle clicked into place.

With a snap of her fingers, Kate said, "That's what she meant when she said her ex-husband set *them* up in her swanky condo."

"When she said it, we both assumed she meant for the two of them," Jane added, "which is why we figured he'd be showing up there."

"Well, sadly, the little guy was born with methamphetamine in his system, and with no father listed, little Charley went into foster care," Abbey told them. "Mom had supervised visits, and had to submit to random drug tests."

"She couldn't get her son back until she was clean," Bill said. "That makes sense. When did she get him back, and are we assuming Luke is the father?"

"He is not listed anywhere official, but he was born between Luke's 2nd and most recent stint in prison. They were divorced after he went in the last time," Abbey answered. "As far as the parentage goes, well, you're the detectives, but I will add that Tonya ended up completing an addiction recovery program at Banyan Treatment Facility about six months ago. It is a private, very exclusive center that costs more than she could possibly afford."

A fancy rehab, and a nice condo in the suburbs, all paid for in cash, checked plenty of boxes for the team. It wasn't a stretch for them to believe that Luke was the child's father given how the dates lined up, but Jane had to wonder where all the money was coming from, and why?

"One last thing, crime fighters," Abbey said, "Tonya's story has a very happy ending and I love happy endings. I know you have to follow the case where it leads, I just hope none of the ugly touches her, or Charley. She never missed a visit with him, and even when she was at the rehab center, little Charley's foster mom brought him for visits. Tonya was released a little over six months ago and was granted her full parental rights shortly after that."

After Abbey signed off, the task force concurred that they did not believe Johnson's early release and abundant cash flow was a coincidence. It was discussed in detail what his connection to the killings might be, and what he may have done to earn that kind of money. Not for the first time that day, Jane wondered at the possibility of her father's involvement, and pondered the benefits of coming clean with her team.

Sam came in with a notebook and interrupted the quiet deliberation of the task force.

"I spoke with the officer who responded to the car accident, and he had a lot of questions, too, but his efforts to further investigate were thwarted by his commanding officer."

"What were his thoughts and concerns?" Patrick asked.

"Apparently no one witnessed the crash, so it wasn't until the next day, when someone reported the busted-out guardrail that authorities were even contacted. They searched the area with their patrol boat and found the car submerged about 500 yards upstream. When they pulled it out of the water, they found the victim still in his seatbelt." Sam paused to turn the page in his notebook, and then continued.

"What the officer found strange about it was that there was no sign the driver even tried to stop, and that it appeared he made no effort to free himself. He wondered if perhaps the guy was dead before he even hit the water, but his wife, through her attorney, refused to allow an autopsy based on religious beliefs."

"Let me guess," Seth commented, "their lawyer was Sal Faraci."

Sam imitated a finger gun and pointed to Seth, "Well, sort of. It was an associate attorney at Faraci's firm. The officer requested the vehicle be checked for possible tampering, but by the time the bureaucratic paperwork was in order, the car had been crushed at a salvage yard."

"So, another dead end," Patrick said, "but not a coincidence either. We need to find Johnson."

Like a seventh inning stretch, the roomful of agents and police officers all stood to shake their numbing legs and refresh their coffee. Jane wasn't sure who made it happen, but whomever kept the coffee pot full and fresh felt like a fairy godmother. With the sustenance their caffeine infusion provided, Bill walked to the front of the room to recap and conclude what they'd learned.

"Our goal for today is to tug hard enough at what we have so we can at least begin to see a bigger picture. Seth and I are going back to Johnson's duplex and push the landlord. He may know where he hangs out, and then we're going to lean on Faraci."

Seth chimed in and added, "Faraci and Johnson are in this up to their necks somehow. Maybe if we push the lawyer with questions about the witness's so-called accident, we can sweat some information out of him."

"My thoughts exactly," Kate said, "Jane and I will go and see Tonya again. We may have a little more leverage now that we know about Charley. It makes sense that if he is Luke's son, and is paying all the bills, that she would have an idea of how to reach him."

Bill nodded in agreement, and then told Sanchez to stay and work with the locals at trying to find some connections and tracking down any traffic cameras they haven't already reviewed.

"That white van is bound to show up on one of them," he said, "so keep studying the videos."

Jane was beginning to think she was the only one to pick up on Sanchez's rigid posture when he was given an assignment, almost she thought, like he thinks they're demeaning, and beneath him. Her thoughts went dark again when she realized that while he was an agent on loan for this case only, he may well be the one to take her permanent spot on the team. Jane thought about the text messages she'd gotten and once again considered that Sanchez could be responsible for them, but she could find no reasonable motive, or determine what his end game was. Could he be in touch with my father, she wondered, and could the reason be as simple as an elaborate setup to make me lose my spot on the team?

Jane shook her head clear when Kate raised her voice.

"I said, are you ready to roll, rookie? Where was your head just now? Because it sure wasn't in this room."

"I'm sorry," Jane answered. "I was thinking about Tonya, and Charley. I really hope they're just innocent bystanders in this mess."

The answer seemed to satisfy Kate, but as they walked out of the building, Jane decided that once the case was solved and her secrecy came to light, she was going to share her misgivings about Sanchez with Bill and Kate.

CHAPTER 25

DAY THREE – 2:00 PM

Rural land – Oakland County, MI

It's been nearly 15 hours since I dumped Eve's lifeless body at the side of the road. I came home and tried to rest but could not ease the turbulence inside. Not even my good friend, Jack Daniels was able to take the edge off. I was slightly pacified when I visited the dark web and learned how to adjust the dosage of my cocktail based on the size of my playmates. I suppose I can't be expected to know everything so soon in my career, but damn it, I feel cheated out of that third day. Not being able to enjoy the final moments with one of my girls felt like having the roller coaster stop at the top of the highest hill. The thrill of that final drop made the anticipation during the slow and steady ride intoxicating and worth the wait, but without it, I just felt hollow.

My mentor and killing coach would caution me to tamper my impulsivity because by acting without a plan I'd likely get sloppy and leave a trail, and besides, the stalking and the hunt are essential components to the torture and kill. Knowing, even days before they become yours, that you hold the power over their life and death is as exhilarating as watching their eyes lose their light. And he isn't wrong, but if I want to be prolific in my own rite, doesn't it stand to reason that I develop my own trademark and write my own epithet?

Mesmerized by the sight of my barn and the empty torture pit inside of it, I attempt to allay my thirst for another playmate, by calling to mind how far I've come as a man since my contact with Tad began. Before my parents died, they told their friends that their only son lived in his computer world because he was too brilliant for normal social exchanges, and it was true. None of us realized at the time that it was one of the many hallmarks I shared with true psychopaths. The old adage that says if you had it to do it all over again fits me like a glove, because I would not have denied myself the pleasure of killing until I was 58 years old. It's the only thing in my life that has brought me true, unadulterated joy.

When I was put on the FBI task force hunting the Mother Killer, I thought I'd finally have the chance to shine, but I was shunned by the team and left out of any real fieldwork. Because I was just their computer consultant, they never even addressed me by name. The information I provided them was a key factor in identifying Tad Wilkins, but when I wasn't recognized for the breakthrough, I decided I'd find my own spotlight and contacted Candace, the intern reporter trying to make a name for herself by following the case.

The premature release of the article caused quite the melee in our unit, and the chief was on the hunt to find the leak. The task force knew who their perpetrator was, and based on the timeline he'd followed, had decided to take a slower approach to arresting him in the hopes of tying him into several other murders. They also wanted to look further into his 15 year old daughter's life in case she was complicit, or a partner to his crimes.

The breaking news from an unnamed source forced them to assemble a team for an immediate breach of Wilkins's home without the planning it usually took for a takedown that size. I was not invited to go, but my hero worship of OMK began on that day. My first insight into my own deviancy came when I empathized with the killer and not the victims, nor did I feel any compassion toward his daughter when I saw her fold up like an accordion in the driveway.

I didn't even think it strange that I identified with the man in the handcuffs and was overwrought with sadness that his reign had come to an end. My resolve to get to know Tad Wilkins became an obsession later that day when my unit chief summoned me to his office.

The man was so enraged his face was a ghastly ash color, as if his fury was so intense it stopped the blood flow. His temper erupted when he told me that because of my breach in conduct, my FBI career was irrevocably damaged, and that I had three choices. I could resign, I could be terminated, or I could accept a lateral move to a Resident Agency in Greenlee, AZ – population 8500. I knew I needed to accept the exile and stay in the FBI if for no other reason than to have access to information on Tad, and to keep an eye on his daughter, Jane. After 10 years of keeping my head down, I made it back to the cyber terrorism unit in D.C., and met the misogynistic, Adrian Sanchez. I didn't know it then, but the female-hating agent would one day play a major role in my new life.

My angry stomach interrupted my reflection, and when I looked at my watch, I understood why. It had been nearly 24 hours since I'd put anything in it besides Jack Daniels, so I shook myself off and hopped into my van thinking about a greasy hamburger with some onion rings.

I took a seat at the bar because instead of a mindless sports program; they had the news on the television above it, and the anchors were discussing my favorite topic – me. Hearing in public about how I baffled even the FBI was one of the many exciting adventures I've had since my new life began. The thrill I felt at sitting amongst the staff without them realizing they just served food to a killer was invigorating. I divided my attention between the news and their conversations as they wiped tables and stocked their coolers.

A waitress, whose name badge read Sandy, seemed boastful when she said, "The FBI agents all had dinner here the other night. I served their pizzas, but every time I went back to the table, they got quiet."

"Oh, how cool. Did they seem nice?" another waitress, Marjory asked. "They were probably talking about the case and didn't want you to hear how they're going to get this nut job."

As Sandy emptied the dirty beer mugs into the hot, soapy water, she said, "They seemed very nice, and tipped great. That handsome state cop, Commander Murphy was with them, and so was sheriff Sam, who told me the next morning that it was only a matter of time till they had the creep in a cage, and that he wasn't as smart as he thought he was."

That last comment from Sandy inflamed me, so before I had a temper tantrum and murdered these women where they stood, I tossed some bills on the bar and took my leave. It was time to show them that I am smarter than they think, and even though Tad would advise me against acting out of haste, I knew what I had to do and headed for my hunting ground.

My heart began to palpitate when I saw her ponytail bob in concert with her foot falls as she jogged around a curve in the road ahead. I smiled and nodded my head at her when I passed because I wanted her to notice an older, non-threatening man. Around the next curve I stopped the van and grabbed my black bag before I hopped out and went around to the back doors. With my bag open and at the ready, I held a tire iron in one hand and my phone with the other, so when I heard her feet pounding the pavement, I was able to curse loudly at the phone I held in front of my face.

"Come on phone, I only need a minute of battery to call AAA." I could hear her panting as she came to my side, which put her in a perfect spot for what I had in mind.

"Do you need to use my phone?"

I smiled shyly and took the offered device but swung the tire iron with my other arm and caught her right behind the knees. In her panic she tried to crawl away, but I planted my foot firmly on her back and soaked the rag with my special cocktail. I didn't want to linger, so I tempered my excitement while I dosed her unconscious, and zip tied her wrists and ankles. After I tossed her into the van, I quickly removed the battery from her phone, and dropped it into the full gasoline container I kept in the van. A less effective killer might have just crushed the battery with the heal of his boot, but I knew how skilled the crime scene techs were and as always, I left nothing behind.

According to the driver's license inside her phone case, my newest treasure was 19-year-old Kacey Caldwell, and she was a real beauty. When the van started bumping along the two-track leading to my compound, she started to stir, and when I saw the blood starting to pool around the zip ties, I knew I was back in my own skin. The invisible, brooding man was gone, and the confident hunter I've grown into felt alive again.

As I dropped my thrashing captive to the stained concrete floor of my torture pit, my adrenaline high crashed and I knew I needed to rest before I could play.

"Miss Kacey, I'm sorry to drop you and leave, but I must sleep now. You should do the same. We have a big day ahead of us."

CHAPTER 26

DAY THREE – 3:00 PM

MSP Incident Center

Sanchez watched the videos on slow motion but didn't register any of what he saw. Instead, he focused on keeping his simmering anger from boiling over when he thought about being kept out of the field again in favor of Jane.

One of the traits he was most proud of was his ability to design a plan, and then to move it forward in a logical order. He developed that skill in college when his slow and methodical course of action proved he was the superior offspring. His patience with knocking his nemesis down, however, was beginning to wane. He had dug as deep as possible into Jane Wilkins/Newell's life, and with the exception of an old boyfriend, was unable to find anything he could use to annihilate her career.

He accepted the offered partnership because he was promised information that would help, but that intel had yet to be shared. He was, however, comforted to know that Jane more than likely felt vulnerable because she knew something was coming her way. She had to be teetering on the edge of stability not knowing what it was, or where it would come from. He liked that he was responsible for how her eyes darted from side to side at their briefings, and how visibly uncomfortable she became around him. Maybe I can just make her lose her mind, he thought, which will get her kicked out of the unit, or perhaps that's been my partner's plan all along.

With that thought, Sanchez came to the decision that it was time to put his dark web skills to good use and find out exactly who the anonymous ally was, and who he was working with. With some of the information he'd sent, including a nickname Sanchez never came across in all his research, he suspected it was someone close to the family, which caused him some concern. But that search, along with an email to Judy would have to be done from the hotel. Tracking anything back to him would be difficult, if not impossible if he was someplace he could bounce his signals off multiple towers.

He could send a text to Jane from his burner phone though. He remembered the text from whomever the third party is suggesting he go for Jane's weakest link, so he did.

Hello again, Janey. Just one question for now-shouldn't you be back in VA taking care of your only family? Talk to you later. :-)

Sanchez smiled a real smile after he sent it, and as he pocketed the burner, his bureau phone rang. Caller ID showed it was Bill, so he answered it right away.

"Sanchez," he said, and then listened as his boss told him that a woman was just reported missing, and that he needed to grab Sam and get to her parent's house right away.

"Sam," he hollered across the room, "we have to leave. Another girl by the name of Kacey Caldwell has gone missing. The count-down on another life begins again."

CHAPTER 27

DAY THREE - 6:00 PM

MSP Incident center

Bill interrupted the chatter in the briefing room when he and Seth walked in.

"Ok, everyone, take a seat and let's find out where we're at. As you've all heard by now, 19 year old Kacey Caldwell went jogging this afternoon and hasn't been heard from since. Seth is going to explain what this deviation in the unsub's method means."

Seth hung his jacket on the back of a chair and explained that Kacey was younger than the other victims, not married, or a mother, and still lived with her folks.

"What this tells us," he added, "is that our killer is devolving, probably because Eve died too soon, and not by his hand, so he grabbed the first female he saw. This abduction was not planned, and she was not stalked, so our hope is that he made a mistake, and we'll find her before it's too late."

Jane sat quietly and tried to keep up with the briefing. The text she had received earlier had her stomach tied up in knots with worry and more regrets that she hadn't told Bill or Kate about her visit with Tad. She relaxed a little after she called Aunt Judy from the privacy of an empty ladies room on the pretext of checking in on her kitten. Her aunt showed no signs of duress, and when she told her that she and Isabelle were going on a getaway to Virginia Beach, Jane was relieved.

Bill took over at the front of the room and told them all that they didn't get anything new or helpful from Johnson's landlord, and that Faraci's office was shuttered and empty.

"We asked Abbey to check into that for us," Bill concluded. "The dark, empty office building without any signage indicating they'd moved doesn't feel right."

Kate replaced Bill and explained what she and Jane learned from Tonya.

"She grudgingly admitted that Charley is Luke's, but for some reason he is afraid to make it known. Luke told her that both she and their son would be safer and better off without him in their lives."

Jane stood at her seat and contributed to the briefing, "At first it seemed that Tonya was nervous, and hanging on by a string, but when she held her son, her whole demeanor relaxed. That baby is definitely her anchor, and neither of us felt like she was consciously aware of anything nefarious."

"She did admit," Kate added, "that she had concerns about how Luke was able to afford her condo. I think maybe she was trying to convince herself as much as us when she told us that Luke told her he'd come into family money."

Jane grinned at that, and concluded, "By the time we left, she did share her suspicion that his lawyer and Tad Wilkins probably had a hand in the money, but she had refused to ask him too many questions because she didn't really want to hear the answer. Abbey is already trying to follow the money."

Both women sat back down after Kate told them that the only hangout Tonya ever knew Luke to have was Prue's Bar on Huron Street, in Pontiac. Sam and Sanchez both stood up when the ladies were finished, but once again Sam was quicker with his report.

"Mr. and Mrs. Caldwell are frantic about Kaccy because they've been watching the news about how the New Mother Killer was abducting and killing young women who jogged. They said she didn't jog with any regular routine because she takes courses at the community college and works part-time. When she does go out, she takes their road, Ann Street, over to Fish Lake, and down to Houser Road. Once she gets to Hickory Ridge Road, she turns around and jogs back."

"That was good information to get, Sam," Bill told him. "It's getting too dark now, but in the morning we'll send someone to drive that route and look for hide away roads, or a logical point of entry for this unsub."

The task force members all took a minute to update their notebooks and, like Jane, to await further assignments. She felt a changing energy in the room and wondered if, like her, the feeling of getting close to putting all the pieces together and stopping this maniac was the reason. She also knew it was going to be a long night because every resource, every brain cell available was needed to find the missing girl and she was happy to focus her entire being on doing just that. She knew her time on the case, and possibly her career, was quickly winding down, but thought, so was Kacey's, and a successful end to that would justify her means.

When Bill and Seth finished their quiet interlude in the corner, the ringing of the phone indicated a Zoom call from Abbey.

"I did it," she exclaimed when the room came into focus. "I found a debit card issued by Trident Trust Company, which happens to be domiciled in Grand Cayman, issued to Sal Faraci. My stellar reputation is intact because I also found that an authorized user on the account is, you guessed it, Luke Johnson."

"Abs, that's fantastic," Seth said, "are you able to track its activity?"

"I'm not at all offended that you felt the need to ask, but of course I can, and did, and I'll go you one further and tell you that just 30 minutes ago a cash withdrawal was made at a bar in Pontiac."

"Was it Prues Bar on Huron Street?" Bill asked her.

"Hey, you stole my grand finale, but yes, it was. And I'm still digging into that 160 acre parcel. Stay safe my lovelies, Abbey Louise out."

The mental stamina in the room skyrocketed with that call, and Jane could almost feel the uplifted spirits within the group. She felt so energized that she ignored how Sanchez's focus seemed to be on stifling a yawn and looking down at his phone.

"Ok group, that is great news, and probably the best piece of intel we've had since this case began." Bill announced. "Seth and I are going to take Sam and go get Johnson at the bar. I'd recommend you get some dinner because once we get back, things may move along pretty quickly."

The three gentlemen grabbed their coats and left the room with a new spring to their step. Sam looked very excited to be a part of it, Jane thought, and he deserves to go. When they first met him, they thought he was just a small town sheriff, but after working with him, they'd all come to respect his ability and instincts.

Kate walked over to Jane as she was putting her notebook and water bottle back into her bag. "We should order pizzas and soda for everyone, and just hang out here. I don't want us to miss the interview. Between Bill and Seth, you'll be able to see two of the most experienced interviewers in the bureau."

"That sounds great," Jane replied to Kate, and then said to the team, "what does everyone like on their pizza and what kind of pop do you want? Our treat."

"Boy, it didn't take you long to revert back to the wrong way to say soda." Coming from anyone else, Jane would've taken that as the joke about the Midwesterner's reference to the soft drink it was intended to be, but from Adrian Sanchez it just sounded snarky and rude, so she ignored him. "I think I'm going to take the Ford and go back to the room for a bit," he added, "I'll grab something on the way, but I need a little downtime."

No one in the room seemed to pay him any mind as they gave Kate their preferences on the pizza, but Jane was grateful he would be gone. Without him lurking around it was much easier for her to focus on the case and not worry if he was behind the text messages, or what his intentions were. And while her action did not show it, Jane felt a loyalty to the team, and knew that regardless of her personal outcome, she owed it to them to share her misgivings.

Almost as if on cue Jane heard the buzz of an incoming message on her phone that she desperately wanted to ignore, but Kate heard it as well.

"Better get that," she said. "It could be about the case."

Jane walked on what felt like wooden legs toward her bag and tried to think of a logical lie to tell, just in case it was from her mysterious adversary. When she picked up the phone, she was a little surprised but not worried about sharing it with her friend.

"Wow," Jane told her. "It's from Nick. I haven't heard from him since I left for Quantico."

"Nick Richards, your ex-boyfriend?" Kate asked. "That's random, what the hell does he want?"

Jane laughed and told her that he just wanted to check in and make sure she was doing well, although she did find it rather curious that just the other day she was questioning if Nick could be the one behind her ambiguous text messages; but like her misgivings about everything else going on, she put it aside to focus on the case.

CHAPTER 28

DAY THREE - 8:00 PM

Quality Inn Hotel

Sanchez was relieved to be away from the incident center because he had nothing to add to the investigation. He blamed Jane for his obvious exclusion in anything related to solving the case. He knew from the minute he got on the plane three days ago that she was going to be the bane of his existence and decided it was time to end the game. He was starting to believe that the mystery man, or men, who'd promised information to thwart her career had no real information that would aid in that quest.

He obviously had his own agenda, Sanchez thought, but I'll be damned if I'm going to be the chump that helps him. This mission is about me, and my needs. The thought that someone tried to use Sanchez for his own personal game, angered him almost as much as that bitch, Jane. He felt his agitation ease when he took his laptop out of the closet and hooked it up. He knew that once he learned the identities of the other players, he'd be able to turn this whole game back to his favor. But first, he thought, an email to Judy that was sure to put a chink in Jane's armor.

Dearest Aunt Judy, have you been keeping up with your niece while she's on the road? Are you aware of just how much danger she's in, and by extension, that you're in? Has she shared who she's been in contact with? Do you even know your niece, or the secrets she holds?

That sent, Sanchez accessed his dark web contacts, and went to work identifying the person, or persons, behind his messages. With the computer doing its search, he took some time to check the hotel's safe. His plan B was ensconced safely within it, and ever since he had facilitated his family's financial ruin, he had never left home without it. He had even outwitted the forensic accountant they hired to bust him, but having a safety net was an imperative piece of his wellbeing.

As he pursued his alternate ID, passport, and unobtrusive list of numbers from his offshore accounts, he wandered back in his mind to how he had made it all happen. His parents did not start out wealthy. His dad was a mechanic, and his mom was a cook in the school's cafeteria. When Adrian would compare their backyard camping vacations to his classmates' lavish trips, he'd be chastised by his parents and told to be more like his sister who never complained. If he wanted a better life, they told him, then he better study hard and get a scholarship into a good college.

As the years of just getting by went on, Sanchez learned that the best way to get along in his family was to just go along. He learned he could quell his angry resentment if he avoided relationships with his peer group and ignored his parents' reminders of what a Latin beauty his baby sister was becoming. He paid no attention when other people commented on how her silky black hair matched her eyes and tawny complexion. All he ever noticed about his sister was how her eyes would gleam when she tossed her hair over her shoulder, because it never failed to turn her audience into putty.

He focused only on getting out of a house he always felt like he was just visiting. Going away to college was how he would make that happen, and he knew his future was going to be in computers. He delivered papers until he saved enough money to buy a secret, refurbished laptop, then grinned at that memory because he still had a secret laptop. It was just newer, with many more capabilities.

Their modest life ended soon after Adrian's high school graduation, when for her 15th birthday a family friend gifted Lacey a $5.00

lottery ticket that had the winning numbers for what at the time was the state's largest ever jackpot. Lacey was too young to claim the winnings, so his parents, who were once hard working and humble, dressed in their Sunday finest to claim their cash out winnings of over 5 million dollars. Lacey, decked out in lace with shiny black patent leather pumps went to the state lottery commission with them, because, of course, with her beauty their newspaper pictures and on camera appearances would look better. Adrian was not invited to go along.

Sanchez took a break from memory lane to check his laptop, but the search was still running, so he thought back again to what he later learned at the Bureau, was his stressor. His parents quit their jobs just as soon as they had the money, and moved into a bigger house in a better school district for the princess. He was getting ready to go off to college and didn't care where they lived, because he had no intention of ever going back. He did hope that he'd be able to give back the loan he was forced to take for his tuition, but his request for money was immediately dismissed by his father.

Sanchez learned by the tuition conversation that his parents would not allow him to benefit from the family's windfall, so he decided to approach his baby sister about getting a used car to take to school. When she flicked her hair over her shoulder and lifted her disingenuous black eyes in an innocent smile and told him no, he knew his family needed to be taught a lesson, and he was able to use his refurbished laptop to do it.

Slowly and very methodically, Sanchez started transferring their money into various accounts he'd set up offshore. It was an exercise in patience for him, but so worth his time, and his brilliance at covering his tracks would be bestseller material if he ever penned his process. He didn't leave them in complete poverty because they owned their fancy house and new cars outright, but he did ensure that he would never go without and that his parents, and even the princess, would have to get jobs if they wanted to eat. Once he had access to large sums of money, it seemed easy to make the connections he needed in order to secure his alternate ID.

Sanchez smiled proudly when his laptop tinged an alert that indicated it had completed the search. He was excited about getting quality information to help put an end to Jane's dream career, but then shuddered when he realized that with her dark hair and eyes, she reminded him of his sister. He hated the female agent because her feminine wiles allowed her to not only best him at Quantico, but to take the spot on an elite team of which he was more deserving. The slight resemblance she shared with his other female nemesis did not really factor into his desire to squash her career. Well, he thought, the cunning female guile *is* what fuels my misogyny, but it has molded me into the man I am today and served me well, so my plan will move forward.

Sanchez walked over to the in-room sink and added ice and another splash of Jamieson to his glass, then re-entered the string of code he needed to access the dark web information. His eyes flashed wide open when the saw the name in bold text on his screen. His mouth fell open and he sat in silence until his throat felt like it was clogged with a dry ball of sawdust. Gulping the rest of his drink Sanchez pulled air deeply into his lungs and tried to absorb what felt like an earthquake at seeing Lloyd Tally's name as the person who claimed to be his ally.

Unsure if his shaky legs were from guzzling a glass of Jamieson or finding out who it was that claimed to be an ally, he replenished his drink and stood at the window. Tally was the closest thing to a friend and confidant he'd ever had, and the fact that he was the one to recommend Sanchez compete with Jane for the coveted assignment on the team sent him back to his laptop for more information.

While the computer did its work, Sanchez leaned back in the swivel chair, plopped his feet on the desk, and replayed all he remembered from his time in cyber with Tally. In hindsight, it seemed clear that Tally's interest that he compete with Jane had more to do with a personal level, and less to do with encouraging a friend to go after what he wanted. It seemed to Sanchez like some dots were beginning to connect, and that his impression of a third person being the one actually in control, was spot on. For the first time since he began his crusade against Jane Newell, he was concerned at what he may have walked into. Have I been duped, he wondered, and led unwittingly into something far more sinister than my desire to tank her career?

He took a deep breath and entered his dark web credentials once more, and then waited as the results from his deeper dive began to appear. Much of his requested information was encrypted, even to him, but he was able to assimilate enough to realize that the nut jobs that had been communicating with him were doing so to orchestrate something far more than he bargained for.

It wasn't too far of a stretch when his information revealed that Tally was in communication with someone in prison, to arrive at Tad Wilkins as that contact.

"Holy shit," he said out loud to his empty room. "Is Lloyd Tally our unidentified subject?"

Resigned to the idea that life as Adrian Sanchez might cease, the agent took comfort in knowing that because of his brilliant planning his plan B would allow him to live in financial comfort for the rest of his life, wherever he chose to live it.

CHAPTER 29

DAY THREE - 8:00 PM

MSP Incident Center

As Jane and Kate cleared away the empty pizza boxes and soda cans, Kate got a text message from Bill that they were on their way in. That Luke never even balked at coming in for questioning was an indicator that he did not fit their profile of the killer.

"You profiled a killer who loved what he was doing and was just getting started," Jane pointed out. "Does it make sense that he'd come in without any resistance?"

"No, it does not," Kate answered, "but we'll know soon enough. They're walking in the door right now."

The two ladies watched from the coffee room as Sam, with his hand cupped under the suspect's elbow, led him into the interview room. The small, scraggly looking man was exactly how Jane had pictured him. His hair made her think of how recently removed dreadlocks might look before a shampoo, and his long beard looked like it would be a friendly breeding ground for insects. But despite his obvious lack of hygiene, there was something almost sad about the way he shuffled alongside the sheriff.

Seth poured his coffee, and when Patrick and Sam joined their group, he told them that the bartender, who happened to be Prue, pointed out Luke who was drinking coffee on a corner barstool.

"We approached slowly and with caution," Bill told them. "We really didn't know what to expect, but as suspects go, he was the most compliant I've ever encountered."

"Which is why we're confident he is not our unsub," Seth added. "We didn't talk to him in the car, but as we said earlier, we're convinced he knows something."

Jane and Kate stood back and listened as the two lead agents strategized how they would handle the interview. Jane listened intently to their planning session and tried to absorb it as completely as a new sponge takes up water. What an opportunity to have squandered, she thought. To learn from the best was like being given a gift, so Jane once again strengthened her resolve to soak up as much of it as she could.

"The audio and video are all set up in the room," Sam told them. "We'll be able to observe, and listen in real time." He seemed genuinely interested in watching how it all went down because, like the rest of them, he was fully engaged in the hunt for the murderer. As any ranking police officer would, especially one from a small town, he took it personally that it was happening in his town and was committed to ending it.

"Okay, we're all set," Bill said. "Let's do this."

The outside group took their places behind the one-way window as Bill and Seth entered the room, and advised Mr. Johnson that the interview was being recorded, and that he had a right to an attorney.

"Do you understand these rights as they've been read to you, Mr. Johnson?" Bill asked.

"Yep, no worries. I don't need no lawyer 'cuz I ain't done nothin' wrong."

It was agreed that Bill would start with the soft, non-confrontational questions, and Seth would step in once a heavier hand was needed.

"Tell me about Charley," Bill requested. "We know that he's your son, but according to your ex-wife, you don't want anyone to know that, and we're curious about why."

"Charley is the only thing good I ever done, and he's better off without me. Safer, too."

"Explain what you mean by safer," Seth requested. "Are you worried your connection to your former cellmate, Tad Wilkins, will cause him harm?"

Luke's tone was louder, and more confident when he answered, "No way. Tad is the nicest and most gentle man I ever known. He took me under his wing and called me a disciple right from the day I went in. He'd never hurt my boy."

The outside spectators looked to Jane after that comment, but her flat demeanor remained because she knew, as did everyone else, that the Mother Killer was a master at making people see him exactly as he wanted to be seen. They noticed the two agents in the interview room exchange glances before Seth continued.

"Okay, we're going to table the conversation about Wilkins for later, but tell us how you were able to afford Sal Faraci, send Tonya to an expensive rehab, and pay cash for a condo in the suburbs? Your financials read like a page out of a book on how to survive poverty. The welfare system just doesn't pay that well."

Johnson lowered his head, uncapped a bottle of water, and after scratching at his scalp, finally answered.

"Tad hooked me up with Sal 'cuz he said I wouldn't survive prison life and needed a good lawyer. The second time Sal came to see me, he told me and Tad that an old aunt died, and I was the only blood relation. Said she was loaded, and all her money came to me."

Jane suspected that her fellow watchers, as well as Bill and Seth, were beginning to get a clearer picture of a man whose own wife called him 'thick in the noggin' from drugs.

"He clearly worships Wilkins," Kate said, "and believes everything he was told."

Their attention was drawn back into the interview room when Bill began to speak.

"That must've been quite a shock. Did you know this aunt?"

"Never heard of her. My old man left when I was born and my momma was drunk all the time, so I didn't know any of our kin. Momma died five years ago of that liver disease."

"Well, I'm sorry for your loss," Bill said kindly, "but if you have all that money, why haven't we found any record of it and why are you still living poorly?"

"I don't want none for myself. It's all for my boy and Tonya. Tad said I shouldn't have control of all that money 'cuz it'd kill me, so he had Sal set it up so as Tonya and Charley would have what they needed. Said he wanted to meet Tonya, and if he thought she had a chance, he'd let Sal pay for a swanky rehab joint. Tad is the smartest man I know, and he was lookin' out for us."

Bill told Luke they were stepping out for a minute, turned off the recording equipment, and joined the team on the outside.

"Well, Luke Johnson is clearly another victim of Tad Wilkins." Bill said, and then added, "He worships that man and truly believes what he was told. Let's go back in and finish up. We still have a lot of work to do."

The two men went back into the room and started the tape again. Jane enjoyed watching how the veteran agents seemed to work in total sync with each other and realized that as experienced as they were, they did not take any short cuts around the legalities. Deviations to proper procedure was not acceptable. The system worked, but only if you worked it and she was disappointed in herself that she'd learned that important lesson a little too late.

Seth started the second phase of questioning. "What can you tell us about being freed from prison before you even went to trial?"

"I dunno," Johnson answered. "All's they told me was that the witness changed his mind, and without him, they didn't have no case. I was sorry I had to go, though, 'cuz I had a lot more learnin' to do from Tad."

The group behind the one-way window, and the agents inside the room all exchanged knowing looks because they knew they'd hit another dead end.

"Let me ask you this," Bill said quietly. "Have you heard from Tad since you've been out?"

The group all sensed the first lie of the night when Luke looked down and without elaboration or explanation just said, "Nope."

"Can you tell us where you were on October 12th…" Bill didn't get a chance to finish his question when Johnson answered: "Don't matter what day, or time, I was at Prues. He has a room upstairs he lets me crash in, and I don't like the dump that Sal got for me, so I stay there. Call him. He'll tell ya I ain't lyin'."

As if he knew it was coming, Sam stepped away from the window and called the bar. They all knew that if his alibi held up, they'd have no choice but to cut him loose.

"Okay, while we check on that," Seth said, "did Wilkins ever ask you to do anything for him, or to contact anyone when you got out?"

The parties on both sides of the window, and even the suspect, went silent after that question. This seemed like their last hope, and with the clock running out for Kacey, they were feeling a little desperate.

Luke jolted the entire group when he slammed his hands down on the table and sat up straight. He looked the men squarely in the eyes, and with more clarity than he'd shown all evening, said, "I'm done talkin' and I know my rights. Either arrest me and call Sal, or gimme a ride back to Prues."

The heads of all the law enforcement officials turned toward one another in shock at the difference in their suspect's demeanor. He reminded Jane of a lost puppy when he shuffled in and struggled to make eye contact, but seemed to find his voice and confidence with his response to the last question. He also showed his hand to the investigators that he did in fact have something to hide. Ferreting that secret out, however, would prove to be the challenge.

"His alibi checks out," Sam told the crowd. "Prue said he's hardly left the place since he got out, but has been back on his corner stool, and in the room above the joint, every single night."

Kate sent a quick text to Bill that Johnson's alibi checked out, but Seth wasn't quite finished with the man.

"Let me tell you about the man you worship. Tad Wilkins is serving multiple life sentences for torturing and murdering 15 young mothers. That is 15 kids who have to grow up without their moms, so when you choose the next person to look up to, you might want to ask a few more questions. Those women were just like Tonya, and had babies just like Charley."

Luke Johnson remained mute as Bill helped him out of the chair and led him out of the room. Seth's final words resonated with Jane, and the rage she felt earlier when viewing the poor women intensified and cemented her choice to stay on the case. FBI career be damned, her determination to catch the New Mother Killer was now unyielding. She'd deal with the fallout, but if Kacey was returned home and the demon was caged, she'd feel good about her choice.

CHAPTER 30

DAY THREE – 10:00PM

Ionia State Penitentiary

To be honest, I must admit that it's getting tiresome to be the only person who knows, recognizes, and acknowledges my greatness. I don't even surprise myself with my grandeur anymore, and while it's said that grandiosity is a hallmark of abnormal psychopathy, I see nothing abnormal about it. I've been this way since I was a boy, and it is normal – for me anyway.

My plan is moving along quite well, and the few deviations from my original script have been dealt with easily enough. Taking matters into my own hands and contacting Sanchez myself was brilliant. He hates Jane, and while his personal grudge is on a much smaller scale than mine, his own venomous crusade to ruin her falls in line quite nicely – which is exactly how I'd written it.

The role for my former cellmate has also gone precisely how I planned it to go. My contacts have informed me that, as planned, he was taken in, questioned, and then released. Of course he was released; he was telling the truth as he knew it to be, so my daughter and her elite team were unable to garner any help from him.

Luke being placed in my cell was random, but grooming him into a disciple was sheer brilliance. To put it nicely, I'd consider Luke's brain to be uncomplicated, but in truth he's not firing on all cylinders, and it was clear from the very first day that he was desperate for someone in his life he could look up to and emulate. That yearning of his made the choice of masks I wore quite simple. I was going to be that man, and by the time he walked free it was like I'd cast a spell on him. He worshiped and honored me as his higher power by the time he left.

This new Mother Killer, on the other hand, has to go. His usefulness to me has expired, and if I've learned anything, it is to eliminate loose ends because as sour milk will make you sick once its reached the expiration date, loose ends could destroy you.

Before I leave the library, I need to send a message through The Dewey Blog, because I need to initiate Luke's help one last time, and if he remembers his training, he'll know to check the blog often for my messages. I just hope he'll be up to the task, and while I know he'd never deny me, my plan for him might be too intricate for his simple mind, although he does seem to be able to follow instructions if they're listed simply, and in order of execution.

Also, in the interest of being a good sport, I'm going to contact my soon-to-be former protégé. It seems only fair, in light of his adoring infatuation of me, that I let him know personally that I'm breaking up with him.

As I walked past the old guard sitting at the librarian's table, I nonchalantly took the black sharpie pen he left out and slid it up my sleeve. I nodded to him that I was ready to leave, and put my hands behind my back. All inmates are shackled while in the hallways and common areas of the prison. The shrill blare of the opening gate was so routine that I no longer flinched at the sudden noise, but stood quietly and waited for the gentle prod from the old man and proceeded to the kitchen for my night shift of cleaning.

I don't enjoy cleaning up after a group of filthy derelicts, but it is the most efficient way of getting a message to the outside. I write the code for the Dewey Decimal System Blog in black marker on a trash bag which is picked up by one of my contacts and passed along.

It's worked well for 13 years, so after bagging up the filthy dregs left by the miscreants, I slid the sharpie out of my sleeve and wrote **025.431** at the top of it as a message to the trash collector, then put the marker in the trash bag, tied it up, and tossed it down the chute to be picked up.

Chapter 31

Day Four – 6:00 AM

Rural Oakland County

I woke up early today with a smile on my face and a spring in my step, which judging by the empty Jack Daniels bottle, seems miraculous. While I waited for my coffee to brew, I stepped out on my porch and inhaled the crisp morning air. Watching the first blush of the morning when it peeks over the horizon is something I've come to relish and appreciate for the promise a new day represents. Its magnificent red-orange ball of fire as it starts to awaken and gleam in the reflection of a cloudless sky used to be as invisible to me as I was to the world. On mornings like this, when I have a playmate waiting just 300 yards away, I feel like a sunrise with the promise of bright new day.

While I am anxious to start playing with Kacey, I'm not going to rush in there this morning. I've learned that the longer you hold them isolated and bound on the cold concrete, the more terrified they become. The dirty rag I tie around their mouths are drenched by their own saliva, and their wrists and ankles are raw and oozing from their fruitless struggle. Best of all, though, is how they plead for mercy through the abject terror in their eyes.

The full indicator on my coffee pot illuminated at the same time the audible alert on my computer buzzed with a new email, so I poured a cup of the strong brew and unplugged my phone. Tad was the only one with that email address, and if he held true to his methods from my training period, I would need the temporary user ID and password he always texted in order to access it and I was eager to read it. I was expecting praise from him because of how well I'd lived up to his image, so when I read his note I was flabbergasted. I would even accept his criticism because his daughter's career hadn't imploded yet, but the harshness of his words really threw me off.

Hello Lloyd, I felt I owed it to you to let you know personally that you're fired. To be clear, you are no longer a protégé of mine, and further, you are not worthy of being called the New Mother Killer. You've disappointed me in many ways, and while I'm happy to have given you this opportunity to fulfill your life's calling, I must also tell you that you are nothing more to me now than a loose end. If you remember your training, you will know how I handle loose ends.

Candidly yours, The Original (and only) Mother Killer.

I read the message three times before I shot up out of my seat and began to pace. My disbelief grew into an anger so intense that it seemed to flood my chest and pound at my composure. Heavy feet marked my every step as I inhaled sharply and tried to calm my pulse, because as sickened as I was by his words, I knew I needed a clear mind to process them and decide on a plan moving forward.

My thundering steps eased and my rapid breathing became tempered when I realized that Tad, as much as I once idolized him, was not in control of my new life. I felt almost relieved that without his direction I would be free to control my own destiny. I would always be grateful to him for opening my eyes to the wonderment of holding one's life in my hands. As sure as the morning sun promises a new day, I will continue to live as I was destined to live. His veiled threat about loose ends did call for more contemplation, but today I would show him and the FBI that I will never be exiled again. I would prove that I was no longer in his shadow, and would make it known that I would be more prolific than Tad Wilkins ever dreamed of being.

As I changed out of my sleepwear, I finalized the plan I hatched. I would surpass the world's view of OMK's heinous quotient when I successfully captured, tortured, and murdered two women at one time. Holding and then disposing of two women was far riskier than just one at a time, but I was excited to conquer that challenge. It would be what set me above all the rest, and would pull me from living unseen in the shadow of others.

As I turned the key in the oversized padlock on my barn door, I looked at my watch and congratulated myself on my timing. This was the optimal time of the morning to find a lone woman jogging on the back roads. Between school bus runs was always my first choice, but I'd gotten my routine down so well and was so quick, that I was sure I could adapt to the change.

The screech of the rusty door as it opened had my latest captive straining her neck back between her shoulder blades. The hope of salvation in her eyes was replaced almost instantly by terror-stricken pleas when she realized it was the monster responsible for her torment.

"Good morning, Miss Kacey. I'm sorry I can't stay and play right now, but I'll be back soon, and will bring you a surprise."

The young lady managed to flip herself over to her stomach, and slunk along the concrete like a worm, groaning for release through the gag in her mouth. They all attempted that worm-like slither, but stopped when they realized all they were doing was rubbing their skin raw beneath the zip ties, and that their captor actually enjoyed watching them suffer.

"I just need to re-stock my black bag and I'll be out of here. You are free to scream and thrash all you want, but it will do you more harm than good. We're in the middle of nowhere, so those muted grunts will not be heard, and the more you struggle now, the less energy you'll have for later when we play."

I was thankful I'd filled my thermal mug with coffee as I left the sanctity of my remote compound, and headed for my hunting ground.

Tad's dismissal, and even his threat to me, was not even on my radar as I bounced along the dirt road looking for the woman who would help elevate my newfound career to new heights. As luck would have it, I saw a bouncing auburn ponytail at about the same point in the road as I'd spotted Kacey. Perfect, I thought, as I passed her with a smile and an uplifted coffee mug.

I pulled off at almost the same spot, and followed the same routine that worked so well last night. I had my phone in front of me when I heard her heavy footfalls, but after taking her offered phone, and swinging the tire iron, I heard a hissing sound and involuntarily shut my eyes.

"What the hell," I shouted as I rubbed at the burning liquid and gathered my wits enough to swing wildly with the metal rod toward the fuzzy silhouette in front of me. My swing went wide and missed, and with the speed of a ninja and the power of the Hulk, my new playmate kneed me. As I was holding my crotch and falling to the ground, her long leg and dirty sneaker extended from her side and caught me in the jaw.

As I fell to the ground, I realized that the little lady in front of me was no lady. In the twilight stage, before my world went dark, I imagined how I could make her pay for her aggressiveness once I had her in the torture pit.

CHAPTER 32

DAY FOUR - 7:00 AM

Quality Inn / MSP Incident Center

As was planned late last night, Jane and Kate met with Bill and Seth in the hotel's space off the lobby where the continental breakfast was served. Jane was comforted with the solidarity and cohesiveness her group demonstrated whenever they gathered. Whether it was before dawn or after midnight, their dedication to the job was admirable. She looked at them and grinned at the predictability of their appearance. Kate always looked runway ready, and Bill's suit with his coordinated tie were always perfectly pressed. Even Seth's crisply pressed Levi jeans and collared polo shirt was comforting, and she felt content by the way the team always presented their very best.

Jane greeted them all, and then made a mental note to call her aunt when the time became more reasonable. She knew Aunt Judy was fine and enjoying a getaway with Isabelle, but hearing her voice would help ease her anxiety about the last text message she'd received.

Jane skipped past everyone lined up at the counter because she was not interested in making a waffle, and chose instead a container of plain Greek yogurt and of course her coffee. At the next station she added fruit that the placard promised was fresh to her Styrofoam bowl. I can mix this in with my yogurt and be all set, she thought. As she made her way to an empty table her attention was drawn to Kate's concentrated face as she answered her ringing phone.

Jane heard Kate say, "Wow, this is a lucky break, we'll be right there." Then she said to the team, "That was Patrick. Our killer tried to grab another woman today, but she got away. She's at the post, and they're waiting for us."

"Well, I suggest you grab something you can eat in the car because we have to go," Bill said, "anyone hear from Sanchez this morning?"

Jane put her yogurt and cellophane wrapped spoon in her messenger bag and told the group that he'd just gotten off the elevator.

"We can grab him on the way out," Bill said. "Let's roll. If she can identify or describe the man, it could be the break we need to bust this wide open."

Jane followed Kate through the lobby, where she paused only long enough to tell Sanchez why they were rushing out the door. Jane was pleasantly surprised when he fell into line without any of the arrogant commentary she'd come to expect.

Jane noticed that the front end of Bill's Expedition seemed to lunge forward when he rammed it into park, just as theirs did when Kate positioned her truck beside them at the police post. They all hopped out and rushed into the building without any concerns of falling into one of the crater sized holes. The buzz of excitement Jane felt when they first learned of the woman who escaped was evident inside the station as well. Jane felt like her skin was tingling and wondered if this was how it felt when a case was about to end, or if the feeling was of gratitude that a potential victim managed to get away. Either way, the natural buzz she felt was a feeling she knew she'd chase for the rest of her life, one way or the other.

Patrick and Sam met them at the coffee pot, and while the commander seemed to be hanging back and conferring quietly with Kate, Sam briefed the group.

"The lady's name is McKenzie Kendall. She's 21 years old, has no kids and lives with her boyfriend in them apartments over by Quick

Road. Village Square, I think they're called. She's pretty shook up, so we gave her some coffee and she's waiting for her boyfriend."

"What time did she come in?" Seth asked.

Patrick set his coffee cup on the table and answered, "She ran in just three minutes before we called you. She always leaves her car at the beginning of her jogging route, so she ran back there and drove straight in because she didn't have her phone. We called her boyfriend from here."

Bill broke off from the crowd and walked to the door when a young man walked in. Their voices were muddled, but Jane could tell by his agitated stance and the way his head rotated from side to side as if searching for something, that the man shaking Bill's hand was McKenzie's boyfriend. Bill ushered the gentleman into the coffee room and introduced him.

"Everyone, this is Alex Turnpow, McKenzie's boyfriend. Alex, these are the men and women who are going to find the man who tried to abduct McKenzie." Alex nodded politely, but it was clear all he wanted to do was see his girlfriend.

Seth stepped up and shook the man's hand, and then in a calm and reassuring voice, told him that they would take him to her immediately and give him a minute alone with her, but urged him to please not ask her to tell him what happened.

"It's vital," he said, "that we get her story, from the beginning, while it's fresh. The details are what is going to catch this guy, and we've found the most effective way to do that, is by hearing it told for the first time, from the witness."

Alex nodded his understanding as the team made their way down the narrow hallway. Patrick opened the door for him, and the group watched through the window as McKenzie leapt into his arms.

"Sam, I'd like you in with Seth and I when we talk to her," Bill said. "You are familiar with the roads and are a local. She may feel more comfortable with you than with us."

Sam acknowledged his statement as Bill continued, "The rest of you can watch from here, and if I feel we need a female's touch of compassion, I'm going to call you in, Jane. Are you okay with that?"

Jane smiled, and felt more than okay with the idea; she was hopeful for the opportunity. As the three men entered the room, she reflected on everything she'd learned the last three days, and more, on how her education since she made the choice to withhold the details of her prison visit had increased tenfold. And for that experience alone, even knowing that her actions could end her FBI career, she was grateful.

"Hi McKenzie," Bill started. "My name is Bill. I'm with the Federal Bureau of Investigations, and Seth here is my partner." Seth smiled at the woman, and Bill continued, "The third gentleman joining us is Holly's chief of police, Sheriff Sam Childers."

The thousand-yard stare of shock McKenzie had when she walked in was gone, and since she'd seemingly gained her composure, Seth started out by asking if she would walk them through her morning.

Grasping on to her boyfriend's hand, McKenzie began: "I like to run on Belford Road because it takes me by the Great Lakes National Cemetery. My uncle is buried there, and it always brings me comfort to see all the American Flags and the memorials honoring our country's heroes."

McKenzie drew in a deep breath, and continued, "I heard a vehicle behind me, but didn't give it too much thought because I was far enough over for it to pass without a problem, and it did. It was a white van and the man driving it was older. As he passed me he smiled and held his coffee cup up as if in a salute to my efforts. I smiled back and waved, but by that time he was around a curve and out of sight."

Jane looked around at her teammates and knew they shared her empathy toward the trauma this young woman was about to relive, but they also seemed impressed by how well she was holding up.

"When I rounded the curve, I saw him standing at the back of his van. He had his phone in his hand, but down by his side I could see he was holding something close to his leg with his other hand. It looked like a pole or a rod of some sort, but it made my skin tingle enough that I slowed my gait and took a can of pepper spray out of my pocket. I didn't feel right just running past the old guy in case he really needed help, so when I heard him hollering at his phone's dead battery, I stopped and offered him mine."

Sam told McKenzie to take a minute and offered her a bottle of water. Both she and her boyfriend seemed grateful for the momentary reprieve, and after guzzling half the bottle she took a deep breath and went on with her story.

"I kind of had my side eye on his other hand, which was a good thing because as I handed him my phone, he raised his other arm and swung it quickly toward me, so I aimed my pepper spray and let loose on the trigger."

"That was amazingly quick thinking, and gave you time to run away," Bill said.

McKenzie offered a hesitant half smile, and replied, "Actually my aim was a little off. I hit him a little below his eyes, but it was enough that he knew something wasn't right and swung again with the metal rod." She broke eye contact then and spoke almost embarrassingly at the table. "Luckily his swing was off because it gave me time to knee him in the junk."

The agents on the other side of the glass snickered at that comment, and leaned into the window to hear more as she raised her head back up and spoke directly to the three men.

"I have been practicing Karate since I was six years old, and earned a black belt when I was 15. When he grabbed his crotch and started to crumble to the ground, I pivoted and placed a high, sidekick right to his jaw, which took him all the way down. And then I ran like hell back to my car."

Having obtained a Level 5, brown certification in the self-defense system of Krav Maga, Kate told them that having the skills necessary to earn that level is a remarkable feat, but possessing the level headedness to use the skill when threatened as McKenzie was, was impressive. Jane watched as Kate spoke because she knew her friend spoke from experience.

"I didn't even take the time to grab my phone, I just ran away as fast as I could and didn't stop till I got to my car. Hell, he could've been lying unconscious, or even dead for all I knew, but I wasn't going to take the time to find out."

All three of the men in the room were shocked silent and watched as the adrenaline that gave McKenzie the energy to tell her story crashed, and started another wave of shuddering sobs. McKenzie's boyfriend wrapped her in a hug and used his shoulder to absorb her salty tears. It was Sam who seemed to gather his wits the quickest and told her that her quick actions, and of course all her training, had most definitely saved her life.

Bill came forward with a box of tissue and asked McKenzie approximately how long ago it happened. Jane assumed the team thought as she did that if he was kicked unconscious, he might still be out there.

Through her quivering lips, McKenzie replied, "I'm not certain, maybe an hour, tops?" Then she added, "It seems a lot longer, though."

Having already learned the exact location of the attempted attack, Bill turned toward Patrick at the window and nodded his head. When the commander barked at the deputies to get out to the spot, she knew they were all of the same mind.

"Call the CSRU on the way," Patrick added. "Have them meet you there. Even if he took off he may have been in such a hurry that he left something behind."

Bill took the seat beside McKenzie and asked if she remembered what he looked like. When she that she felt she could describe him, he asked her, "Would you be able to wait for a sketch artist? If he's who we think he is, he's already murdered three women, and is holding another one captive right now."

McKenzie's face blanched and her eyes went wide as if it finally clicked that the man who tried to abduct her was the killer she'd been hearing about on the news. She took a nervous gulp of her water and told them that she would wait as long as Alex could stay with her.

When they came out of the room, Sam told them he was going to the donut shop in town, and Patrick told one of the officers to contact the sketch artist and get her there ASAP.

"I'll grab some bagels, too," Sam said. "I know I need more than coffee, and those kids might want something while they wait."

Jane once again felt her respect, and fondness for the sheriff grow. He was perfect for the job he had, she thought: competent, and yet caring to what he referred to as his folks. She was quiet as she watched the hustle and bustle of the police post as the officers from the night shift briefed the daytime crew before they went home. Jane joined the team at a table in the coffee room, and with the chance finally presenting itself, took the yogurt out of her bag.

"What an amazingly composed young woman," Bill said as he added cream to his coffee, "I hope this cream helps temper my stomach acid until I get some food to absorb it."

"So, this sketch could be a huge break," Seth said, as he too added some cream. "We should get it out to the press right away."

Kate set down her cup and replied, "I agree, someone has seen this guy."

Jane nodded her head, and added, "Maybe we could get a stock picture of a white panel van and put that out there, too. I'm sure there are thousands of them just in Holly, but it may trigger someone's memory."

As Kate started to commend her for the idea Jane's phone rang, and when she pulled it out of her bag caller ID showed it was her Aunt Judy, so she stood up and excused herself.

"I'm sorry," she told them as she walked away, "but this is my aunt, and I really should take it."

In just the instant it took for her to sit at another table and accept the call, Jane's mind ran amok with worst case scenarios. Obviously, she hadn't buried her stress over the last message she'd received because her face began to perspire, her breathing became short, and her hands trembled as she swiped the arrow to answer the call.

"Hi, Aunt Judy. Is something wrong? Why are you calling me? Is Isabelle okay?"

The questions came as rapidly as her thundering heartbeats, but she sat and quietly tapped her foot when, after assuring her they were fine, Judy told her about the email she'd gotten. Jane realized she owed her aunt an explanation on the turn this case had taken when she learned that her visit to Tad was intimated in the email. The many layers of this case, including her trip to the prison, needed to be unraveled, and she fully intended on peeling them all back, but knew she needed a focused mind. Her priority in this moment was a candid conversation with her aunt because she'd been unwittingly pulled into it, and deserved to hear the truth.

Jane took a second to regulate her breathing, and then asked her aunt to put her phone on speaker so Isabelle could hear it as well. Once Isabelle acknowledged herself, Jane reassured them that she was not in danger, and then told them about the copycat killer and her unsanctioned visit to her father. When the line went silent she could almost picture the stunned and worried faces on two women she knew loved her as deeply as she loved them.

When Judy asked her if she thought it was Tad sending the emails, Jane responded, "I'm just not sure anymore, and the truth is that I've gotten several mysterious text messages as well."

Jane became conscious of her aunt's anger when in a brusque voice she asked her why she hadn't elicited at least Kate's help. Judy's distressed tone and how she managed to cut right through the murky details with a simple question seemed to awaken Jane to the realization that so much more than an end to her career was at stake.

Knowing her only choice now was complete and total transparency, Jane answered her.

"When I left the prison, I had every intention of telling Kate what I'd done, but things started to move quickly with the case and I didn't get the chance."

Jane's aunt called her out on that by telling her that it was an excuse and not a reason, so she admitted to the ladies that as the hours passed, the implications of Tad's words, as well as the messages she'd gotten, seemed less threatening. Jane also acknowledged that she felt like she'd finally found her place in the world, so she made the decision to keep the secret just until the case was solved, and to use the time she had left to absorb and learn everything she possibly could.

The conversation quieted after that declaration, so Jane buried the niece mentality, and became an agent again.

"I need you to stay at that resort until I get back to town, which won't be too long because we're getting close. Do not go anywhere alone, and don't answer your phone if you don't know who it is. Put the do not disturb placard on your door, and do not order room service. There should be no reason anyone would come knocking."

Jane took a long drink of her coffee and a deep breath before she told them, "After we hang up I'm going to come clean to my boss and Kate. Threatening my family, regardless of how veiled that threat is, is not okay and we will find out who is responsible." With the compassion and unconditional love back in her tone, Jane's aunt voiced her concern over the loss of her career with the bureau.

Jane did not hesitate to tell her that her career with the FBI meant nothing if it meant that family would be put in harm's way. "I will always be a champion for justice, be it with the bureau or a local police department, but I am who and what I am because of you. I will never risk your wellbeing or your right to feel safe. I will call you as soon as I get the chance, but please do what I told you to do."

CHAPTER 33

DAY FOUR - 8:00AM

MSP Incident center

After the call ended, Jane stayed at the table and gazed out at the bustling station. She knew what she needed to do, and while she had hoped to see the case through, she realized that she could not allow evil to touch her aunt. She also brought herself to terms with the fact that her wicked father might be involved on some level and that the best and probably only way to get to the bottom of it all was with the help of the team. She still couldn't reconcile what Tad's motivation was, however, or how Sanchez played into it, because she felt certain he had a hand in at least the messages she'd gotten. To make me crazy, she thought, or to ruin my career, or both?

Jane's pensive reflection was interrupted when Kate plopped down into the chair across from her. "What's up, Jane? You've got that million miles away look again. Everything okay with your aunt?"

Jane smiled at Kate's candid approach and stood up. When the two women reached the table with Bill and Seth, Jane took a slow and deliberate deep breath, then asked if they could meet in the empty conference room down the hall. Kate gave Jane a questioning glance as if she was trying to dig into her head for answers.

"Thank you for meeting with me in here," Jane said as she quietly latched the door closed and took a chair across the table from them.

She took a bottle of water out of her bag and opened it before she got started.

"This isn't easy to say, so I'm going to get straight to it. I've kept things from this team because I didn't believe they were germane to the case, but something has happened that disputes that theory and I realize that it was never my call to make."

Jane started at the beginning with the text message she received the first night, and continued the confession in a linear order. When she told them about her visit to the prison, their eyes went wide and their mouths gaped open, but they remained silent. She could hardly bear to look at Kate because if betrayal had a look, Kate was wearing it, and Jane didn't have the mental capacity at that moment to deal with it. She concluded with the call she got from her aunt that morning and then accessed the notes file on her phone, handing over the copies of the messages she'd gotten, including the forwarded email from Judy.

The hushed atmosphere in the room prevailed while they passed the phone around, so Jane watched through the window as the uniformed officers went on with their day. As her eyes traveled, she noticed Sanchez dart out of her field of vision, as if he was lurking and watching her from the hallway. His quick movement reminded her that she wanted to share her misgivings about him with the team and figured this was as good a time as any to do that.

"I also want to share some misgivings about Adrian Sanchez, and I may be wrong, but he is the one I've suspected of sending me the messages all along. Those steely eyes of his seem to follow my every move, but my instinct about him is that he is hiding something."

"That was a hell of a load to drop on us at this point in the investigation, and we will talk more about it, but for now, please close the door on your way out. I need to speak privately to Kate and Seth."

Jane nodded her head and did what she was told. She wished she could be a fly on the wall so she could hear her fate. She was also a little surprised at how relieved she felt after having shared the burden she'd carried for three days, and felt confident that with the help of the team she might finally learn who was behind all the messages, although she was as concerned with the reason behind them as she was with who was doing it. The messages clearly contained information only her father, Nick, or, as much as she hated to believe it, another agent would know.

Jane unscrewed the top on her water bottle, and with thoughtful reasoning, decided to tap into her refined sense of intuition and try to connect some dots. Her first thought went to Nick and the breakup. She remembered having a sense of something being off with his reaction to her acceptance into Quantico. She believed him when he said he feared for her safety, but looking back now with a clear head she realized that his fear seemed irrational, and actually, more personal. Her anger at his forbidding her to accept the coveted spot overtook that intuition though, so without ever delving deeper into his motivations, she cut all ties. Jane wondered what made him so fearful that for the first time in their relationship, he was anything but supportive of her dreams. The connection was needle thin at best, and she still didn't believe that he'd go to such extremes to hurt her, but decided to mention him to Kate and the others and let them determine if it was a worthy thread to tug.

Jane took a drink of water and looked around. Her leaders were still behind closed doors, and thankfully she did not see Sanchez creeping around. Her instincts that he wasn't who he appeared to be started on the plane and were stronger than ever. She had no doubt that not only would he have the skill set to pull it off, but his primary unit was in cyber, so he may have been able to access the original Mother Killer case file for the personal information. But she still could not reconcile the reason why he'd be so intent on hurting her. Jealousy seemed possible, but who would go to such extremes over envy? She wondered.

Jane was happy when dark thoughts and intuitions about her father were interrupted by a woman entering the station house. Her crepe-like skirt fell in loose folds to her calves, and with a blousy bohemian top layered over it, Jane was reminded of a modern day hippy. Her no-fuss messy bun, and high-top Birkenstock shoes revealed her to fall more in line with a naturalist. Her soft-spoken voice and friendly demeanor when she spoke to the officer manning the front desk was one Jane immediately warmed up to.

"Good morning," she said as she pushed an errant hair out of her eyes. "I'm Gail. Commander Murphy asked if I could help out with a sketch. Is he around?"

That perked Jane's ears up, and she paid close attention to the conversation between her and Patrick, but no longer being sure of her place on the team, or if she even had a place, stayed in her seat. From their conversation, Jane gathered that Gail was a local artist, who had had much success doing suspect sketches for all the surrounding municipalities. The soft-spoken cadence of her voice, combined with her loose and flowing ensemble, in Jane's point of view, paired perfectly with an artist and she felt sure that their witness would feel comfortable during the process that would surely be a traumatic retelling of her encounter.

Jane's anxiety peaked when she noticed Bill's mission-oriented gait heading her way.

"Will you join us in the conference room, please? We have a few things to go over with you."

Jane felt like her cottonmouth would prevent her from responding verbally, so she just nodded and fell into line behind him. Bill's facial expressions seldom wavered, so his untouched composure provided no hints to Jane as to what she was about to encounter. As she gulped a drink of water, she reminded herself that she made her choices with the full knowledge that she was risking her place in the Bureau, and prepared herself to accept responsibility for her actions. It was actually hearing Kate's imaginary voice telling her to be brave, to stand tall and to fight for what she wanted, that had her squaring her shoulders and raising her chin as she walked into the room and took a seat.

Jane realized in the few seconds between when she sat and when Bill started speaking, that a bond had formed with the three people before her, and even though her heart felt crushed at Kate's refusal to make eye contact, the cohesiveness she felt in this room was worth fighting for.

"First, I want to tell you that we have put a unit on your aunt's resort. Both she and Isabelle are aware of it, and I personally reiterated to them all the safety protocols you'd already advised them to follow."

"Thank you for that," Jane responded. "I appreciate the Bureau's help."

Bill straightened the papers on the table and handed Jane back her phone before he continued.

"Time is our enemy here," he said, "and we can't afford to use what time we do have figuring out what to do with your situation, so having said that, know that this isn't over, but the case absolutely has to come first."

"We've determined that we will be able to put it away for now," Seth declared. "Do you think you can do the same?"

Jane looked straight at Kate with her reply. "I'm certain I can, and I need to assure you all that I will spend the rest of the time I have on this team rebuilding your trust."

"Okay, then let me tell you where we're at." Seth said. "We are still very confident in our profile of our killer, but think we may have been approaching it from the wrong angle."

"When I argued the case to the director for bringing you on the team," Bill told her, "I did so because I thought you might have a unique perspective; but honestly, you've fit so well into the investigation that we all forgot you were raised for fifteen years by the Original Mother Killer."

Jane noticed Kate's stare soften a little at Bill's statement, but wasn't exactly sure how to process his words. She turned toward Seth when he continued.

"We've got Abbey digging into all your texts, and to your aunt's email, but we are beginning to wonder if Tad is playing a larger, perhaps even a main role, in the new killings."

"I've been fighting that instinct since I met with him and he revealed information I didn't think he should have," Jane told them. "I never really believed that from a prison cell he'd have the power to engineer something like this."

Kate spoke for the first time since they reconvened and explained that while it was uncommon, it wasn't unheard of that an inmate as intelligent and well known as Wilkins would maintain connections with the criminal underworld.

"If you really think about it," she added, "and with what we've both learned about him, it wouldn't be a stretch to believe that Tad Wilkins would ever relinquish the power he holds so dear, even being locked up."

Seth picked up where Kate left off and stated, "His whole mindset has always been about manipulation and control. It's what gets him off. I have a couple of questions that might not be easy for you, but are necessary for us to move forward."

Jane agreed to answer the questions honestly and to the best of her knowledge, but also reassured them that separating the psychopath from her father had become second nature to her.

"Years of therapy, living with a psychologist, and being best friends with someone who has a master's degree in criminal behavior, has put me in a better position, at least mentally, than a lot of people."

They all smiled, and Seth went on with his questions.

"Growing up, was there anything that set off his temper and made him really angry?"

Jane thought for a moment and replied, "No, in fact his face rarely showed any expression, and he never showed me any affection. If anything, I'd say that displaying anger, or losing his temper, was more of an anomaly. Looking in the rear-view mirror, I can see now that he was over the top solicitous toward me, gave me things I never even asked for. The only thing he ever denied me was a pet, and the day I brought a stray puppy home was probably the only time I saw him lose his temper."

"How did he seem when you saw him in prison? Do you think he felt joy at seeing his daughter for the first time in 13 years?"

Without hesitation, Jane responded with a resounding, "No. There was no sign of joy at all. He still had the same hate in his eyes I saw as he was ducked into a patrol car. His smile and a low, throaty chuckle were presented in almost a mocking way. No, I believe the only joy he felt, was in my discomfort."

Kate seemed to be more engaged in the interview now, and said, "A man like him has no capacity whatsoever to feel love, compassion, or remorse. His only joy comes from power and control, and we believe it's possible that Tad Wilkins has engineered the copycat murders, and the contacts with you, for the sole purpose of hurting you, Jane."

Jane sat quiet for a moment to process the new theory. Kate went on by reminding her that just because he provided his DNA, Wilkins was no dad, and nothing Jane did, or could do, would change him. That gave her the clear head she needed to address the team.

"That makes sense, I guess – but how the hell can we catch him? If he has the ability to pull something like this off, it stands to reason that he also has power with some heavy hitters."

Kate turned to Jane and told her that she should tell them about Nick and let them decide if it warranted any investigation.

"My ex-boyfriend, Nick Richards, has been in contact with me, also. I haven't spoken to him since before I left for Quantico, but he did know my father used to call me Janey and that I hated it. When I think back on our breakup now, I see that his reaction was irrational and that he seemed almost afraid of something if I went. I didn't dwell on it then because we went our separate ways: he to Manhattan to be a big shot in the financial world, and me to Quantico."

Bill thanked Jane for the information and said he'd have Abbey check him out, just so all their bases would be covered. And then he said to the group, "Jane has a valid point about Wilkins, but let's remember that our case is to solve the murders of three women, the abduction of one who is still missing, and the attempted abduction of another. Tracking Wilkins's connection will be handled by a different team."

Bill no sooner finished his sentence when Patrick burst into the room and told them that another woman had been reported missing. As they grabbed their bags and hustled out of the room, Patrick handed them a composite drawing of their unidentified subject.

"He looks vaguely familiar," Bill and Seth said in unison, and told Kate that she and Jane should go to the presumed victim's house, while they stayed back and spoke a little more with McKenzie. None of them even seemed to realize that Adrian Sanchez was nowhere to be found.

CHAPTER 34

DAY FOUR - 8:30 AM

Once Sanchez saw Jane take the others into a conference room and close the door, he knew his gig was up and that Adrian Sanchez's shelf life had expired. When Jane handed the others her phone, he casually retrieved his briefcase and, on his way out of the building, quietly called for an Uber to pick him up. To maintain his cover while he exited the building, Sanchez held his phone to his ear and carried on a pretend conversation. Once outside he kept the phone up for appearance, but walked to the end of the entrance, so he could leave unseen.

Ever since he had wiped his family out of their millions Sanchez had been preparing and planning for this day, and while the reason to flee had changed, he almost embraced the idea of a total makeover and new life. In addition to financial resources that would allow him to live out his life in luxury, he also had hair dye and contact lenses to match the alternate passport and ID he had. He wasn't sure how he'd look when the dark, Latin coloring of his heritage was replaced with a blue eyed blonde, but circumstances had necessitated the change and he felt more than ready. Maybe someplace tropical, he thought, and then chuckled to himself as the car pulled into his hotel, because for the first time in his 32 years, he appreciated his parents.

With no time to waste once he entered his room, the soon to be disgraced FBI agent accessed the information he'd gotten on Lloyd Tally. With what he knew about his former friend and colleague, the man would have no choice but to help him disappear. He knew when he accepted help that this day might come, and although Adrian Sanchez would soon vanish, he hoped the shrewd actions of the underground players would achieve what he wanted all along: to ruin Jane Newell. From what he learned in his research, it became obvious that his personal vendetta was what made him the perfect cohort for someone else's twisted plan, but he harbored no resentment at being used. He wanted them to succeed and finish what he started.

While Adrian emptied the contents of the safe into his duffel bag, he considered the irony of the connection he'd made to the Original and the New Mother Killer case that put he and Jane on the same team. As he dialed the phone, he wondered how far Tad Wilkins's involvement went, and if it was possible that everything, and everyone connected to the case had been engineered by the man serving life in prison.

No matter, he thought, as the phone made the connection, I'll be long gone.

"Hello, Lloyd, it's time we became re-acquainted. I'll expect your white van to pull into the parking lot of my hotel room within the half hour."

As an afterthought, he grabbed the information he'd acquired from the darknet, and with a grin on his face, sent another email through the back channels he'd unearthed. He knew he was making a pact with the devil himself by emailing Tad, but if it helped facilitate Jane Newell's fall from grace, it was worth the risk.

Chapter 35

Day Four – 8:30 AM

Rural Road – Holly Township

It took me a minute when I woke up to realize that I wasn't in my warm cabin, but sprawled out on a bed of damp gravel behind my van with a golf ball sized rock wedged into my neck. In an almost panicked state, I popped myself up to a sitting position, and looked around for the auburn-haired girl I'd set my sights on. Once my head cleared, I grudgingly had to admit to myself that she got away and more than likely was either on her way to, or already speaking with, the authorities. With no time to spare I used the bumper of the van to help myself to a standing position and took a quick assessment of the ground around me. Pleased with myself for having the presence of mind to remove any traces of my identity helped center my thoughts, so I picked up her phone, dropped it into the gas can, and gingerly climbed into the driver's seat.

I drove forward, but kept my eyes focused on my rear-view mirror until I was able to turn off onto another, unnamed dirt road. Fortunately, I'd had the forethought during my training to get to know all of the rural turn offs in this area, many of which were not even maintained by the county.

When I felt comfortable that no one was pursuing me, I lowered the visor so I could take stock of my appearance in the mirror. I was not surprised to see the flaming, purplish-red bruise forming on the right side of my jaw, I was, however, surprised that I had any movement in it. That ninja move the tiny redhead made clocked me well enough to make me lose consciousness, so I can't believe my jaw isn't broken. Her aim was off with the kick, just like the pepper spray failed to make its mark, but her knee to my groin was spot on.

Despite my physical discomfort, I was still feeling euphoric about being liberated from Tad Wilkins. He thought I'd feel dejected and would flounder without his direction, but I'm exhilarated to be on my own, and more, to prove to the world that compared to me the Original Mother Killer was tame. His hooded threat, while intended to intimidate, was no more than a menace and I was not going to allow it to hinder my plan to oust him from his notorious reign. I would do what he never even tried to do and take two women at one time.

The throbbing in my jaw and parts south seemed to subside during my reverie, and as I began to formulate the next step in my plan "Live and Let Die" started playing from inside the console which is where I kept my regular phone. I seldom used that phone and could not imagine who would be calling me on it. My only communication of late had been with Tad, and those always came through on the burner I kept in my pocket. I kept my left hand on the steering wheel, and with my right hand I popped open the console and dug to the bottom for the phone quickly because my ring tone only played through three times before it bounced to voice mail.

The twisting around shot hot daggers of pain through my groin, so with great effort, through a clamped jaw, I mumbled, "Hello?"

The commanding voice on the other end caused the throbbing in my ears to beat in unison to my hiccuping heartbeat because I recognized the caller, and there was only one reason Adrian Sanchez would be contacting me. I started to question him, but he cut me off as soon as I addressed him by name, and directed me to pick him up, then disconnected the call without giving me a chance to question him, or, more importantly, to refuse.

I looked closely around and behind the van, and when I saw nothing but the mature oaks going bare of their vibrant leaves, pulled off into the only spot in the foliage clear enough to turn a vehicle around on the narrow dirt road. He'd given me 30 minutes, and I only needed about 15 of them, so I decided to give this new turn of events some consideration.

I took him on at Tad's direction, and now realized that Sanchez's motives to ruin Jane's life were a perfect match to Tad's, whereas mine had evolved since I became the star struck, chosen protégé. At the beginning, my blind devotion to OMK, and the desire to emulate him drove me to feel as he felt, to believe as he believed, and finally, to kill as he killed. But something happened when I added my own style to the game. Some may call what I did torture, but the artfulness I added to my women could only be compared to the work of a gifted visionary. And after the first time my eyes connected with the eyes of a soul departing its body, my appetite for the act became ravenous; while I'll always be grateful to Tad for showing me the way, my blind infatuation for him is gone. I don't need to follow him anymore. I'll be famous in my own rite.

As I bumped along on the dirt road that would lead me to town I spotted my chance at redemption about 300 yards ahead. She wasn't jogging, but was carrying a dog leash, calling out for Murray, and stepping off the road to the edge of the woods, promising good boy a treat if he'd come. I know a golden opportunity when it's presented, so I grabbed what was left of my Subway sandwich, stopped my van just ahead of her and opened the back doors. In my hand the pretty lady would be able to see a half-eaten meatball sub, but my other hand remained inside and gripped to the tire iron.

"I've never known a dog turn down a meatball," I said as she approached. "Would you like some help looking for Murray?"

I knew I had to time my swing perfectly and throttle her right at the knees so she'd drop and then move quickly on to the zip ties. I'd prepare a rag of my homemade cocktail once she was secure in the van. I also needed to keep an eye out for Murray because I did not need to lose an arm to a dog protecting his human.

When she fell forward, the sub sandwich and the dog leash flew from her hands, and as if she didn't realize what happened, her focus was on trying to reach them, instead of on me. That hesitation in her reaction gave me time to bind her hands and her feet and get her into the van.

"Oh, you're a pretty young thing," I told her as I prepared my rag. "We'll have time for formal introductions later, but right now I have another appointment to keep. Sleep well my beauty."

With the adrenaline rush of my unplanned, yet very successful appropriation of a second playmate, it seemed I'd hit the main road by automatic pilot. I needed to channel my thoughts in these next minutes to Sanchez, and how he could've learned I was the one who promised to provide him with information to ruin Jane's career. Maybe Tad contacted him directly and that was the basis for the threat in his last email. It really didn't matter where he got his intel though; I was rather excited to bring on a partner because it is one other thing that Tad was never able to accomplish with his daughter.

Up ahead I could see Sanchez standing on the curb in front of The Quality Inn with a large duffel in his hands. This was the second interruption in my day, but I've adapted, and if I'm being honest with myself, am excited to show Adrian how proficient I've become in my second career.

When I saw a sheriff's car move into the turn lane of the hotel, I was glad all I'd have to do is slow down enough for Sanchez to hop in. I assumed they had, or would soon be getting a description of my van from the bitch who got away, so I needed to keep a low profile and get it off the roads as soon as possible.

CHAPTER 36

DAY FOUR - 9:30AM

Ionia State Penitentiary

Living inside a prison is much like small town life, where simple chatter was meant to kick start a lively exchange within a group of people desperate for amusement. But to a group of inherently angry men, the gossip inevitably turned to ugly accusations, which in the general population of a prison yard, is dangerous. My fellow inmates know that I don't play, and know better than to try to engage with me. I pay handsomely for quick and honest information, and after making examples of the first few who failed to live up to my expectations, I've been more than satisfied with my sources. Today, however, I was presented with a gift I hadn't even requested because a new, and possibly valuable source for the future, came through for me. Maybe Adrian Sanchez did have a redeeming quality, or two.

The turnaround time from when Janey came clean with her bosses to when I was notified was as close to immediate as it could've been. When I pictured her sitting alone while the powers that be had their pow-wow to determine her fate, I felt a tremendous amount of joy and pride that I'd accomplished my first goal of tanking her dream. I was a long way from being done with the mind games I had planned, but felt confident that my first milestone was met. With my end game already in motion, my checkmate to end this first game was imminent.

Chapter 37

Day Four – 9:30AM

The two women wasted no time grabbing their bags and rushing out of the building to their vehicle. When Jane realized that Kate hopped into the passenger seat, she took her messenger bag off her shoulder and tossed it in before climbing in herself. Without a word, Kate entered the address of who they presumed was another abductee into the truck's GPS, and as they headed toward her house, the only spoken word came through the dashboard with turn-by-turn directions. Jane was glad that the new woman's husband had been paying attention to the news, and as a precaution, called them when his dog came home from their morning walk alone. The sooner they start searching for a missing woman, the better her chances of survival.

One of the most treasured aspects of her friendship with Kate was being as comfortable together in their silence as when they were engaged in conversation. The stillness in the car today felt awkward, however, and almost forced, to Jane, but she wasn't sure what she could say or do that might cut through the fog of tension between them. It was one of the qualities in Kate that she found most endearing that provided Jane with a solution when imagination Kate told her to get to the damn point and say what she meant.

Jane gripped the steering wheel hard, and turned to her friend. "Can we please address the elephant between us? Avoiding it isn't going to help. I know I deserve everything I have coming, so please, lay it on me."

Kate's glare became softer, but her silence felt even heavier to Jane than it did before her outburst, so she toned down her voice and told her friend that she knew how badly she'd let her down.

Finally, Kate spoke: "You don't get it, do you? This isn't about our friendship, and it isn't me personally you let down; we are a team, and you let us all down. As your training agent I am personally responsible for every single move you make in the field. I advocated for you, Jane; campaigned to have you added to the most coveted team in the Bureau, and it wasn't because you're my best friend. It was because I believe you have a skill set, and an aptitude for this work that can't be taught." Jane felt dumbstruck at Kate's words because as many times as she'd considered the possible consequences for her actions, she'd never given thought to the potential damage it could do to her friend's career.

Kate's rise in the FBI was legendary, but Jane knew that the stellar reputation she'd attained, while well deserved, came at a personal cost. Just days before her graduation from the Academy, she went for celebratory cocktails with the other recruits at The Green Leafe Bar, in Williamsburg. In a decision she soon regretted, Kate decided to stay and keep celebrating after her friends left because she had so many reasons to be happy. Kate was as excited to see her entire family as she was with getting through the 20 weeks of intensive training at Quantico. With a Jamaican mother who was as dark as her Irish bred father was fair, Kate and her six siblings joked about being the only piano key family in the neighborhood because their shades ranged from ebony to ivory. But she loved and missed every one of them, and felt blessed that they were all making the trip to see her graduate, while many of her training mates would have no one to stand up and cheer for them when they walked across the dais. She had a few drinks to celebrate with them as well.

Jane knew that the only people who knew the entire story behind Kate's brutal assault that night were Aunt Judy and Isabelle because they were her therapists, although Jane always suspected that the attack was far worse than Kate had ever let on. From what Kate did tell her, Jane knew that Kate's Krav Maga training kicked in just in time to save her life, and that making bad choices while intoxicated were now in her rear-view mirror.

Jane re-centered her thoughts and responded to Kate.

"In the last couple of days, I've rotated through each scenario so many times that it feels like the wash, rinse, repeat instructions on a shampoo bottle. I knew I was risking my career, yet was able to rationalize every lousy choice I made, but I never once considered that I could be putting your career at risk, too."

Kate sounded more like herself when she told Jane that they had to find a way to box it off for now, and to close this case.

"You made a mistake," Kate told her. "Many of them. For a while I was too angry and shocked to even consider how to respond, but I also know that grudges will drag you down forever."

For the first time since she'd gone off the rails, Jane felt a glimmer of hope that if nothing else, her friendship with Kate might recover.

"Bill hasn't taken your badge or your gun yet," Kate went on, "so until he does, you are still an agent on this team. We need to re-evaluate how we've approached the investigation. We've been focused on victimology, but I think we need to profile the other actors in this macabre case."

Jane was comfortable with keeping the case as their safe zone, and told Kate that she agreed with a change in approach.

"While I was waiting for you outside of the conference room, I did try to sort through my intuitions on Nick and Sanchez, but I had a hard time figuring out the why of it."

Jane sensed that she was going to learn as much or more about investigative tools and techniques as she'd learned since they were brought into the copycat killer case. She also knew that being allowed to finish out the case was a gift and planned to focus intently on every detail, every action, and every word moving forward. She didn't know where, or in what capacity, she'd be doing it, but Jane knew beyond a shadow of a doubt that her life's mission was to catch and cage the monsters.

"Okay," Kate said, "we need to map out some connections with the players we know about. If we find the nexus between Nick, your father, Luke Johnson, and possibly Sanchez, it'll put us a lot closer to finding our killer."

Jane felt like she was being led to a conclusion the rest of the team had already made, and told Kate, "With the exception of Johnson, that connection could be me, or even scarier, Tad, but I still don't understand why."

"We don't either, so let's talk about Nick. Dig deep into that big ass, intuitive brain of yours and think about how he was acting *before* you told him about Quantico. I know you dumped him because he acted like a boorish neanderthal and tried to forbid you from going, but was he acting differently prior to that?"

Jane was relieved that the silence between them was back to a comfortable one while Kate gave her time to process her thoughts. Thinking back to Nick's attitude took a great deal of focus because what stood out the most to Jane was her own state of mind.

"Thinking back, I do remember him being more irritable, and I guess distracted," Jane told her, and then added, "but I sort of blamed myself for his moodiness." Jane explained to Kate that she assumed Nick's antagonism was because her every thought was on the Academy and the anxiety she felt while she waited for word.

"I never even told him that I'd applied to the Academy, so I was probably quiet, even withdrawn from our relationship."

Kate seemed astonished with that. "Wait – what? Maybe we need to dissect that a little bit. Why didn't you tell him you'd applied?"

And then, as if playing devil's advocate, she told Jane that finding out the way he did could be the reason he wasn't the supportive boyfriend she wanted him to be.

"No, that wasn't it," Jane explained. As if she'd been struck with an epiphany, she stated, "I just realized part of what really bothered me: he didn't act the least bit surprised when I told him. I just thought he was acting like a petulant child, but I was so caught up in my own excitement that I didn't give it much more thought."

Jane spotted brake lights ahead as cars were forced out of the left-hand lane. She put her right blinker on to merge because no one liked the person who thought their commute would be quicker if they waited until the last possible minute to get over.

Jane saw that Kate had scooted up in her seat and craned her neck to look up the shoulder of the road, and said, "I'm not sure if it's an accident or road construction ahead, but it's starting to back up. Fortunately, our exit is coming up."

"Okay," Kate said. "His demeanor before you were accepted, and the impression you got that he already knew you had applied, is a line we need to tug. When we're finished with this interview we're going to figure out what Nick Richards knew, when he knew it, and most importantly, how he knew it. I'm going to text Abbey his information and see if she can find anything."

Jane agreed with Kate and then told her that both his parents were still alive, lived in Richmond with his younger sister, and that his plan was to move to NYC and take the financial world by storm.

As Jane turned off the exit and approached the house they needed, Kate texted Abbey and then told her that they were off to a good start and would go further after they were finished inside.

Jane nodded in agreement and as she unbuckled her seatbelt, thought ahead to her next mental journey. She knew that delving into her feelings and intuitions was about to get deep and the need for her to detach her personal feelings would become more important than ever before. It wasn't her past with Nick that had her concerned, but the fact that she'd need to dredge up her intuitions and feelings when they discussed the creep that fathered her. She'd spent thirteen years exploring and processing all the ways in which Tad's brand of crazy affected her: before and after his arrest. She had also honed many tools that helped her to put it all away and not allow it to define her.

Imaginary Kate spoke up in her mind again and reminded her that she pulled herself up and all the way into the FBI, despite her crazy ass father, so regardless of the outcome there was no doubt that once again, Jane Newell would stand on top of that bag of garbage, instead of climbing into it.

Jane heard Kate's phone buzz as they stepped out of the house with a dog leash in an evidence bag and a distraught young man watching them from the porch. As Kate took the call, Jane wished she had taken a jacket with her that morning because the weather had gone from unseasonably hot and humid to windy and quite chilly just since they'd gotten to the house.

"That was Seth," Kate said. "They're waiting for our briefing and apparently Abs has some information on that private land."

Jane was happy that the conversation on the way back to the incident center revolved mostly around their interview with Mr. Anderson about his missing wife and the darkening storm clouds that were beginning to move in from the east. When Jane pulled into the parking lot, she and Kate discussed their plan for the briefing.

"I want you to take the lead on this one." Kate told Jane as they dodged raindrops on their way into the building and then commented, "Wow, it's only 10:00 AM and it's as dark as night. A storm must be coming. I can feel the difference in the air."

Jane sensed that having her take lead was Kate's offering to help her reestablish her place on the team. She was grateful for the opportunity to mend the self-imposed rift she'd created, and while she knew it would take more than just a single briefing, Jane felt the confidence boost Kate had extended. As was their routine, the ladies stopped for coffee on their way back to the incident room where the task force was waiting, and once again Jane silently blessed their coffee angel for keeping it hot and fresh all day long.

Jane walked to the front of the room and removed the plastic bag that held the leather dog leash from her bag and smiled inwardly when Kate chose the seat beside Patrick. For the briefest of seconds, she realized she did not have the clammy sensation she usually did when she entered a room with Adrian Sanchez in it.

Ignoring that blip in her brain, Jane jumped right in. "Our newest victim is 27-year-old Vanessa Anderson, and according to her husband of only three months, she left the house around 9:00 to look for their Golden Retriever, Murray." Jane noticed the faces of the task force at the idea of a family dog being lost, so she continued. "Murray came home with the leash in his mouth, but without Vanessa. Mr. Anderson stated that the dog was acting nervous, and kept pacing to and from the door, so he walked to the end of their road and called out for her." Jane took a sip of her hot coffee, and continued, "When he got no response, he got scared and ran home to call the police."

Jane held up her phone and told the group that Mr. Anderson texted her a picture of his wife and that she'd print it out for them as soon as they were finished.

"Vanessa Anderson is a black female, about 5'7, and weighs approximately 165 pounds. She does not do yoga, aerobics, or jog, so there are no connections to the other ladies, which makes it even more obvious that our killer is not after a certain type. We believe he is familiar and comfortable with the back roads, and chooses women of opportunity."

Seth stood up, and Jane's jittery stomach settled when he commended her profile assessment, and said that he was in total agreement.

"What do you make of the leash in the dog's mouth?" Bill asked.

"Kate and I believe that the leash flew out of Vanessa's hands when she was abducted, and the unsub, who we figure had to be running a little scared because of McKenzie's escape, didn't realize it. Or he did, but wasn't concerned with it because it's clear he is devolving."

Jane set the leash and her coffee down on the table, and Kate concluded the briefing.

"Our theory is that Murray either heard commotion, or heard his mom calling for him but found only the leash when he got there. Dogs are really smart, and extremely intuitive; we just really wished that he could tell us what he saw."

Jane knew the group had a chuckle over Kate referring to Vanessa as Murray's mom, and was pretty certain Patrick was ribbing her about it, too. Kate grew up with a couple of goldens herself so she was pretty partial to the breed, and like many dog lovers, chose to refer to their humans by their role, rather than using just a pronoun. The first time Jane met Kate's family, she was introduced to her dogs, Cagney and Lacey, as Auntie Jane.

Bill stood back up and quieted the group's laughter. "We'll get the leash to the lab, but I don't hold out a lot of hope on it. Let's all take a seat now because I'm going to call Abbey for updates on her end of the investigation."

Jane couldn't help but to smile as she walked to her seat because Bill walked beside her and told her he was very pleased with how she handled the briefing.

"Good morning my loves," Abbey said. "You have certainly kept me busy, and I am just as happy as a kitten with catnip to help my fierce protectors."

Jane smiled as she always did when Abs spoke in her lyrical comparisons, and as she studied the faces of the officers racing against the clock to save lives, she could almost feel their tension dissipate. She smiled too, because today Abbey's platinum blonde hair was wound into two, tightly braided buns at the top of her head, and on the earpiece of her headset was a fuzzy pink kitten.

"I have oodles of information for you. First up, I'd like to direct you to monitor number one, where I have the satellite photos of the private land beside the disposal site."

Abbey had a stylus of some sort in her hand, and she drew a red circle around two dark shadows.

"I am sending you the enhanced image of it, but those blobs are buildings, and they look rather large, yet there is nothing in the county records to indicate that this property is occupied."

The group's attention was suddenly pulled away from Abbey to the window, where the total darkness became like a backdrop for an electrical light show with a brilliant, sky-to-ground bolt of lightning. The crackling of the electricity was still audible when the resounding boom of thunder joined the display, and then as quickly as it started, the daytime sky grew eerily dark and still once again.

"Yoohoo, are you still with me my friends? I want to draw your attention to monitor number two because the information there is going to knock you right out of your sensible shoes. I didn't have to go back quite as far as the dinosaur age, but my extraordinary skill has unearthed the person paying the bills on that private land beside the disposal site, so tighten up your shoelaces boys and girls, because that ghost is going to knock you off your feet."

The attention of the group was drawn back to Abbey's screen, but before she gave them a name, another crack of lightening lit up the dark sky, and plunged the entire building into darkness.

A half a dozen cell phone flashlights lit up to a cacophony of grumbling and cursing.

"Are you kidding me right now?" Sam shouted. "Hey Patrick, do y'all have a generator? Ain't no one got time for this shit, especially Kacey and Vanessa."

"We do," he answered, "but it isn't automatic. A couple of the guys will get it set up. We should be good in no time. I just hope the internet comes back with it."

Bill took control of the room and suggested that they spend the down time checking out the images Abbey sent.

"They'll be much easier to analyze on a bigger computer screen, but it's about all we can do right now. If she's able, I'm sure Abbey will text us the name, but I'm guessing that with all the lines down, the cell phone signals will be overloaded and she won't be able to get through."

CHAPTER 38

DAY FOUR - 10:00AM

Tally was disappointed his newest playmate was still unconscious when Sanchez jumped into the van because he didn't even notice her. Sanchez was more concerned with getting away from the hotel as quickly as possible. He warned Tally that thanks to his screw up with McKenzie, the police not only knew he drove a white van, but were probably only moments away from blasting his sketch across all forms of media.

"That may be," Tally said, "but that sheriff's cruiser turning into the hotel was not looking for me. What's your story, *Agent Sanchez?*"

Tally watched and could almost hear the gears turning in the agent's head as he tried to decide what to tell him, and what to hold back. It didn't matter what he told him, because Tally already knew all there was to know about his sad life, and why he was now as much of a fugitive as him.

"My story isn't important," Sanchez shot back. "I figured out you were the one texting me and that you were the New Mother Killer we were hunting. I also know of your other nefarious connections. All you have to do to ensure my silence is help me get out of town."

Out of the corner of his eye, Tally could see movement in the cargo area of his van, and knew it wouldn't be long before his other passenger realized her perilous situation and began the predictable squirm and struggle against her bindings. The gag in her mouth would mute her screams to just pitiful moans, which was always thrilling to Tally, but the best part for him was when their panic-stricken eyes bore into his. The realization of how close he was to that moment brought a smile to his face because he knew Sanchez was about to grasp exactly what he was a part of. As if on cue, the young captive began her fruitless screaming as she fought against the zip ties and squirmed along the grooved metal floorboards of the van.

Sanchez turned toward the noise, then quickly snapped his head forward. After a couple of slow, deep breaths when it seemed as if he'd convinced himself that what he thought he saw was just an aberration, he took a slower look in the back. Tally remained quiet as his passenger's eyes went wide; while he could see the shock on his face, Tally also noted that there were no visible signs of disgust or loathing. He looked at that as a promising sign that a mutually beneficial partnership could be formed.

As if his voice and state of consciousness were awakened at once, Sanchez turned toward Tally and shouted, "What in the actual hell have you done?"

"What do you mean, what have I done? You told me you knew I was the New Mother Killer. Did you think the women just showed up, like old people at an early bird buffet?"

"You are a sick son of a bitch, you know that?" For Sanchez the question was rhetorical, but Tally seemed eager to answer.

"Define sick," Tally said with a chuckle. "Don't think I haven't seen you sneaking looks at our guest. I didn't have time to get her name. Why don't you go back there and take the gag out long enough to ask her. It makes this so much more personal, don't you think?"

Sanchez made no motion to move, but just shook his head as if he was trying to un-see, or at the very least, make sense of what he had seen.

"All I wanted was a place to lay low for a day or two, an internet connection, and a ride to the airport. In no way did I want to be a part of this - whatever this is."

Tally sat quietly and watched Sanchez take a mental journey to sort, process, and most important, forge his own path forward. As much as he wanted him to embrace the calling and join forces, he reminded himself that not everyone was as mentally evolved at the beginning as he was. Tad gave him the boost he needed at the time, but now that he was liberated, he had no doubt that his days of being a sheep and just following social norms would have ended with or without that encouragement. What he needed to do now was show Sanchez how good it felt to shed the heavy cloak he'd been using to masquerade his true character.

Tally noticed a drop in the temperature and a curtain of dark and ominous looking storm clouds. "You're about to see one hell of an electrical storm," he told Sanchez. "I've been in this state all summer and when the temperatures go from hot and humid to cold and windy this fast, you know it's going to get lively."

Indignant at Tally's attempt to redirect his rage, Sanchez asked him, "What in the hell is wrong with you? You have a woman writhing in the back, and you want to talk about the damn weather?" Without waiting for an answer, he continued, "Screw it, I can do what I have to do without your sorry ass. Just take me to a motel out of the way someplace. It doesn't even have to be nice. I just need internet access."

Tally realized then that he hadn't given his former colleague enough time to settle into, and get comfortable with the prospect of controlling beautiful women. But knowing how he loathed the fairer sex, Tally believed that given time, and with enough encouragement, Adrian Sanchez would happily subscribe to a new way of living.

"Whoa, slow your roll, partner," Tally responded. "I have a perfect spot for you to lay low and an internet connection that will bounce you off towers from Guam to Greece, and everywhere in between. There is no need to get nasty."

As he turned off the main road and headed back toward his private compound, Tally pulled the van over as close to the ditch as he could get and climbed into the cargo area. His new playmate was creating quite a racket, so he decided to give her another dose of his magic elixir to settle her down.

"I make this myself, and it works wonders. Our new friend here will settle in for a nice little nap in about 30 seconds."

As Tally saturated the rag, he noticed Sanchez watching him through the side mirror, and decided that once the little lady was unconscious, he'd approach him as if he were a businessman with a sales pitch.

"Listen, Sanchez," he pleaded, "I get that this whole thing was thrown at you rather suddenly, but your call demanding I pick you up forced me to facilitate things a bit quicker than may have been optimal." When Sanchez gave him a dumbfounded look but remained speechless, Tally continued. "I know how much you hate women, and that you've been manipulated by them since your sister was old enough to bat her eyes, and flip her hair over her shoulder. I am offering you the opportunity to vindicate yourself, and reclaim your place as the rightful patriarch."

Sanchez looked appalled at Tally's inference, and asked, "What the hell are you talking about? Yes, I am a confirmed misogynist, but I'm no sadist. I prefer to use my brain over my brawn to take down the manipulative little bitches. I told you before, I want nothing to do with whatever it is you're doing with these women."

Tally grew furious at Sanchez's refusal to partner with him, and as his van bumped along the gravel road toward home, he let him know.

"Tad was right about you," he started. "You are a wimp. You say you use your brain to take down the bitches, but where was that brain when I manipulated you into hating Jane Newell almost as much as her father does, and when I expertly brought you on to her team, the very team assigned to hunt me?" Gape-jawed, Sanchez narrowed his icy gray eyes and stared at Tally, as he continued his tirade.

"You have no idea how good it feels to have complete and total control over someone who wouldn't even notice you in a grocery store." Calmer now, Tally continued, "I'm a little disappointed that you would dismiss it out of hand, though. It isn't like you aren't comfortable with criminal acts, because if you were, you would have already unholstered your gun, or at the very least, called in your team." Tally knew he hit a nerve when Sanchez squirmed in his seat, and focused his stare out the side window.

As he turned onto the well-hidden two track that would take him back to his home and work area, he told Sanchez that whether he liked it or not, he was complicit in the abduction of the still unconscious woman in the back.

"But above all else," he declared, "I am a man of my word, so I will provide you with the safe haven you need – but don't push me. I know you think you're an expert on the fine art of surveilling, stalking, and manipulating on the dark web, but don't think for a moment that you'll be able to fade into oblivion, because I'm better."

Tally could tell by Sanchez's acquiescent nod that he believed him, but because he liked to see people in distress, concluded, "And don't forget that I also know where all your secrets are buried. Now, I'm going to go and open the barn door, and I need you to open the back doors of the van. I may need some help getting the lassie settled."

CHAPTER 39

DAY FOUR - 10:30 AM

MSP Incident center

Jane and Kate, along with the rest of the task force used their phones to study the image of the private land that Abbey had sent over. The storm, having blown violently through the area, ended almost as abruptly as it started. Daylight shone through the windows which helped the group study the photos using their back-lit devices. Restoring power via the generator was delayed because many of the officers were dispatched on storm related emergency calls, leaving the station with just a skeleton crew. The screen on Jane's tablet was bigger than her phone's, so she used that to examine the snapshot the satellite had taken.

"Hey guys," Jane called, "come take a look at this and tell me if you see what I see."

The group gathered behind her, and with her stylus, pointed to a very tiny object on what appeared to be a front porch.

"Does that look like a glass half full of a brownish liquid on what looks to be a small table?" Jane leaned back so they could all get close enough to study it, and continued, "Didn't Abs tell us that although the utilities were on, she found no residency permits, or any other indication that this property was occupied?"

"She sure did," Seth answered. "So if it isn't occupied, why would a drink be on the front porch?"

"That was a good find, Jane," Sam said. "I didn't notice that on my screen, but I hate to be a buzz kill: this image could have been captured anytime."

"That is true, Sam," Jane said as she moved the screen up, and pointed to the bottom right-hand corner of the image, "The satellites pass by, on average, about every 15 minutes, but Abbey must've caught this just perfectly, because it's stamped 102210 / 0700. This screenshot was taken this morning."

"Wow!" Kate exclaimed. "Our unique and exceptional analyst has once again proven her unparalleled brilliance. She must've been on that satellite and caught the still-shot as it passed."

All eyes looked up when the hanging fluorescent lights emitted a faint crackle, and then flickered on. A united cheer could be heard over the whirring beeps of the computer terminals restarting. Jane wasn't sure if it was the generator doing the work, or if the power had been restored from the pole, but it didn't matter: time was running out for Kacey and Vanessa. Finding out what Abbey learned could be the piece that made the puzzle come together.

Bill stood up from his seat in the break room and asked them all to join him in the incident room. "We need to re-connect with Abbey. She has a name for us, and with any luck it could be the break we need to bust this case wide open."

The optimism in the room was palpable as the task force gathered their files and electronic devices and headed into the hallway. Jane quickly rebuked herself at her disappointment in the coffee angel when she passed the empty coffee machine. The power just came back, she thought; give the mysterious good Samaritan a break.

The familiar ring tone of the Skype call snapped everyone in the room to attention as Abbey came into focus on the big screen.

Abbey exhaled in relief when the connection was made, and exclaimed, "Oh, there you are! I was so worried my family had been sucked up in a tornado that I hacked into the National Weather Service to keep an eye on things."

Seth laughed and told her everyone was safe and then reminded her that she did not have to share everything she did in that room of hers.

"You were about to tell us the name of whomever is maintaining that acreage beside our disposal site."

"Oh, yes I most certainly do have a name, and I believe I told you, before we were so rudely disconnected, to tighten up the shoelaces because the man keeping the lights on is a retired agent."

"Please cut to the chase, Abs," Bill said as gently as he could. "We are fighting the clock here."

"Of course, sir. The man is Lloyd Tally, and he retired from our cyber unit in D.C. almost a year ago."

"That name sounds familiar," Seth said. "What else can you tell us about him?"

"He was an agent for nearly 25 years. Started out in D.C., but then was sent to a resident agency in Greenlee, AZ in 1998. He didn't find his way back until 2007."

"Greenlee, Arizona?" Kate asked, "Sounds more like a banishment than a relocation."

The way Abbey's lips pressed forward as if suppressing a grin was her tell that she still had a bombshell piece of information, so Jane knew what she said next was what she promised would blow them away.

"I haven't even told you the best part yet," Abbey said as she pointed her feather topped pencil at the screen, "Lloyd Tally was on the task force that ultimately brought Tad Wilkins down." Abbey allowed that information to sink in before adding, "My people tell me that he screwed up really bad during the investigation and was put in time out for nine years."

Jane watched as the silent group processed what they'd just learned. She was sure that with the investigative skill this team had, they were doing exactly what she was doing - adding some missing pieces to the puzzle. As if their minds really were in sync, Kate and

Jane exchanged a look of clarity.

"Didn't Sanchez come from cyber?" Kate asked.

"And where has he been?" Jane asked when she recalled how the spine-chills she'd attributed to his presence had been noticeably absent since before the storm hit.

Bill looked around in shock and asked Abbey to send over a picture of Tally.

"It's already on your devices," she replied. "Abbey Louise out for now, but standing by."

Bill took charge of the chattering crowd, and asked Patrick to print the photo of Tally for a six-pack of pictures to show McKenzie.

"If she positively IDs him as the man who attacked her, it will be enough to get a warrant on that property. Sam, will you send a deputy to the hotel to find Sanchez? The rest of you, with me in the break room for a strategy meeting. I remember now why the name, and even the sketch looked familiar, and Lloyd Tally definitely fits our profile."

CHAPTER 40

DAY FOUR - 10:30AM

As Tally coasted to a stop between his house and the barn, he told Sanchez to open the back doors and grab his gear.

After he stepped onto the van's running board, Tally told him, "We'll come back for the little lass in a couple minutes. I just want to show you around the place first." Tally couldn't help feeling a little smug at how skillfully he handled Sanchez's self-righteous attitude and quick denial of becoming partners. He knew the agent's career with the bureau was over, and that he'd spend the rest of his life changing identities and moving from one obscure location to another. Tally also knew those measures were necessitated because of his own criminal acts, so his sanctimonious front was nothing more than a hypocritical sham in his opinion.

Tally gained a renewed sense of hope as he walked toward the barn that Sanchez might gain a little more interest once he saw the torture pit, and admired just how well he'd outfitted his work area. The bounce in his step faltered when he got close enough to see that the heavy padlock on the door was hanging open. He'd always been so careful about locking it when he left, so he stood still for a moment and replayed his last visit. In only a few short hours, he felt as if he'd evolved from being controlled like a puppet on a string, to a mastermind in control of his own destiny, and decided that the transformation process might have contributed to a couple of lapses in his routine. He continued toward the barn door with a warning to himself that complacency, or veering from the plan is what put lesser men than he in prison. Not me, he thought; never me.

Tally could hear Sanchez's footsteps behind him as he leaned with all his weight against the heavy door. The screech of it as it scraped along the concrete floor had become synonymous with the grunts and groans of his playmate in the pit, and just as predictable was how the door swung out quickly when its bottom cleared the floor, and practically flung Tally into the barn because he'd been pushing with all his strength when it released.

He quickly regained his balance, but then halted his advance and froze in place when he saw the straggly vagrant that had come to his house so long ago and given him the keys to this haven. His arms shot up when he noticed that the man clenched a gun in both his dirty hands, and that those hands were shaking like the last leaf on an autumn tree.

"Hey buddy, slow down. What the hell are you doing here? If it's money you need, I have plenty. I'll even let you take a turn with Kacey over there, but you need to put that gun down before it goes off." As he spoke, Tally took small, deliberate steps backward, but the crazed gunman kept advancing with the barrel of the gun directed center mass, despite the trembling hands that held it.

The scruffy man seemed to spit as he stuttered his way through what sounded like a scripted response, "I have a message for you, from Tad." Tally extended both his arms in front of him in a futile attempt to halt the man who was threatening his life, while, in what could only be explained as a sudden detoxification, "He said that you should have known how he takes care of loose ends."

Tally had backed his way almost to the opening which would give him a chance to bolt, because he figured that with as badly as the gunman's hands were trembling, his chance at hitting a moving target were slim.

All of a sudden Tally was knocked sideways by a charging Sanchez who must have heard the exchange, and drawn his sidearm.

"FBI," he shouted with his gun out in front of him. "Stay where you are and drop the gun." Tally watched as the intruder stumbled with the shock of a third party, but did not drop his weapon. As Sanchez began to shout another warning, Tally saw his jaw drop in shock when he noticed Kacey slithering like a snake in the torture pit. That distraction was all he needed to tackle Sanchez and take his gun because in that moment, he knew, it was either his life, or the vagrant's.

Tally was impressed to see Sanchez's training kick in after he fired, when he popped up at the blast in time to see the intruder's head jerk back from the impact, and then collapse in a heap with both arms extended at his sides. His gun was thrown from his hand when the bullet hit. By the time Sanchez reached him, the crimson blossom had spread slowly across his stomach, but his rising chest was proof that he was still alive – for now.

"What the hell was Luke Johnson doing here?" he demanded. "What did he want? And is that Kacey Caldwell over there?" Tally could tell that Sanchez was going to demand answers he either did not have or wouldn't want to share, but knew there was no time to debate.

"We'll have time to hash all of that out later, but for now, we need to get the hell out of here. Grab your bag and close the van doors. I need to get my computer."

"What the hell makes you think I'll go anywhere with you?" Sanchez asked.

Tally put the agent's gun in the waistband of his pants, and answered his question.

"Because like it or not, we are now partners. How long do you think it'll take to figure out that a 9mm, FBI issued Glock, was used to shoot that man, huh?" Sanchez's face had the same dumbstruck look he'd seen multiple times since he first got into the van as he continued, "I have an alternate location where we'll be safe, but we can't get the van in there, we'll have to take the Gator, it's all terrain."

"What about Kacey, and the injured guy, and what are you going to do with the girl in the van?" It was clear to Tally that Sanchez, even though he wasn't the one to make the kill shot, knew he had no choice but to comply, but answered anyway.

"Sadly, I'll have to leave the ladies behind. The guy will bleed out soon though because that's what gut shots do – they cause painful suffering while life slowly drains away, but the bastard deserves to die. As far as my ladies, I suppose they'll eventually die, too, unless I think it's safe to come back for them. I worked damn hard to get them, but there's more where they came from."

"You really are a sick son of a bitch," Sanchez said as he slammed the back doors on the van, "now where the hell is your damn gator?"

CHAPTER 41

DAY FOUR - 11:00 AM

MSP Command Center

The walk down the narrow hallway was quiet as the task force headed to the break room for their strategy meeting. The nutty aroma of freshly brewed coffee put a pep in Jane's step, and as she awaited her turn for the caffeinated goodness, she set a mental reminder to leave a thank you note for the mistress of the bean before she left the state. As she filled her large, travel sized mug, Jane surveyed the room and followed Kate's eyes as she watched Patrick walk in. He stopped briefly to talk to Bill and Seth who seemed to be having a private chat near the doorway, before joining Kate at her table.

While she hadn't admitted it, Jane was certain of Kate's attraction to the tall Irishman and that pleased her, because she hoped he'd be the man that would knock down the wall her friend seemed to insulate herself behind. Jane suspected that it all related back to the assault before her graduation, but was respectful of their boundaries, and never really pressed her on it. Of course, she also had to admit that by getting her friend to open up she might unwittingly start a thread of heartfelt give and take, and she was not certain she wanted to engage in the giving part of the exchange. Jane trusted her friend's opinions and advice; she just wasn't sure how deep she was ready to dig.

Kate's hand was waving her over, so Jane's thoughts about

leaving her alone with Patrick were thwarted as she and Sam took their seats at the same time. Bill and Seth topped off their coffee cups and called the room to order.

Bill started off by telling the team that learning an unidentified subject's identity is a giant leap toward stopping his heinous crimes.

"That information from Abbey, combined with agent Newell spotting the half full glass on the porch, are two huge breaks in this case. McKenzie is being shown the photo array as we speak, and hopefully she can make a positive ID. Seth is going to explain what he knows about Tally, and how that information affects our profile." His reference to her as agent did not go unnoticed to Jane as she dug her notebook and pencil out of her bag.

"When we saw the sketch of the man McKenzie described for the artist, we both thought he looked vaguely familiar, but it didn't click until we had a name to go with it, which you all know is Lloyd Tally." Seth went on to tell the group that at the time of the Tad Wilkins case, he and Bill were both assigned to the New York field office, and while they weren't on that task force, they were kept abreast of the progress.

The room was so quiet as he spoke that Jane was afraid the sound of her pencil to paper as she took notes would be as cringing as the sound of fingernails scraping a chalkboard. But with this being her first, and possibly only strategy meeting as an FBI agent, she was determined to take copious notes.

"We became aware that one of the agents, in an effort to make a name for himself and take credit for an entire team's efforts provided information to the press." Audible gasps were made by the group, because it was well known that commenting on an active investigation to the press, or anyone else, was taboo and could be grounds for dismissal.

Seth took a drink of his coffee, and continued, "Suffice it to say that while the information he gave was not inaccurate, it was far too soon to go public and forced the Bureau to arrest Wilkins before they were ready. Having to hastily plan and arm a breach team without the benefit of a well-planned strategy could have had deadly results, but we were lucky."

Hearing Seth talk about it from law enforcement's vantage point was eye opening to Jane. There wasn't a detail of the day that she didn't remember as clearly as if it were yesterday. Those memories are what she believed defined her life as an adult, because when the fog cleared, she was in awe at how the agents and local police departments seemed to have complete and total control of not only her dad, but in quickly removing her from possible harm. That discipline, and precision when arresting a serial murderer, is what drove her toward her goal. To learn that the team had to act without the benefit of a solid plan was almost surreal.

Jane tuned back to Seth as he went on, "We had a solid case on the 15 women he was convicted of killing, but our profile told us that there were many other Wilkins' victims out there someplace. His methods and signature were too defined and too controlled to believe they were where he got his start. Because of Tally's need to be recognized, and our inability to build the case, there are a lot of families that have no answers and have gotten no justice for their loved ones."

As if on cue, Kate stood up and explained that the unit chief at the time was able to ferret out Tally's name as the source, and he was very, very angry.

"At the time," she said, "the FBI was still trying to rebuild its image from the Ruby Ridge and Waco debacles of the early 90's, and the chief did not feel the Bureau could take another hit to its reputation, so he gave Tally the option of either resigning in good standing, or relocating."

Bill stood up to conclude, "He chose the relocation, or banishment as we all knew it to be, and pretty much faded into oblivion. He kept his nose clean and found his way back to D.C. after nine years, where he also stayed under the radar. Honestly, by then we were in the same field office and I never noticed him."

A loud buzz from Sam's phone interrupted the hushed group, so they turned their attention toward him, watching him read a text message on his phone.

"McKenzie just made a solid ID. It's confirmed, this Lloyd Tally fella is our perpetrator. If it's okay, I'll leave and go type up a request for a warrant, and find a judge still available to sign it. Lots of times, if their docket ain't too full, they break off early on Fridays."

Patrick told Sam to go and to keep him posted on his progress. Seth went on to explain that Tally's need to be noticed, and recognized, fit perfectly with the profile they had on him. The group all nodded at how much sense that made, and then Seth, in a quieter, more reverent sounding tone, delivered his final words.

He was addressing the group, but looking at Jane when he said, "In light of what we've just learned, it's likely that Tally was in contact with Wilkins, and perhaps he was even hand chosen, and trained, to become a protégé. We don't know how, or why, but an investigation on how Wilkins may be communicating will be turned over to another unit. Our priority is stopping a cold-blooded murderer before he kills again."

Seth's final words rang true to Jane. As she reflected back to her prison visit, it dawned on her that the uneasiness she felt at sharing space with that monster masked the most troubling thought of all. Tad Wilkins did not seem surprised to see her on the day of her visit; as a matter of fact, he acted as if he'd been expecting her. Jane knew she needed to share that revelation, but not yet. They had lives to save. The reasoning and motivation behind the mind of a deranged psychopath, while important, could wait.

Kate packed up the files she had on the table, and told Jane to do the same, that she wanted to talk to Bill about something.

"Bill," she said, "I'd like to take Jane and head toward the GPS coordinates Abbey sent. It's close enough to the disposal site that I think we could walk in from there."

Jane felt like she knew exactly why Kate wanted to do that, but kept quiet through the exchange between them. Kate explained her concern that while they had little to no information on how Tally was operating, they did know that he was very computer savvy.

"I'm worried he'll find out about the warrant," Kate said, "and rabbit before we get there." Bill was contemplative for a moment before he answered.

"That's a good point, Kate. You two get a head start, and we'll be right behind you, but do not, in any circumstances, breach that private land until we have the signed warrant. We don't want to lose this case in court because we cut corners in the investigation."

"Understood, sir. Jane, grab your bag. You're with me."

Jane hooked her bag across her body and headed toward the door. Her strides, even at a leisurely pace were two to one over Kate's, but as she looked up from the doorway she noticed another reason for the lag. Patrick must have noticed their speedy gait, and stopped to question her. Jane couldn't hear his words, but judging by the giant hand that came to rest on Kate's shoulder, she assumed he was telling her to be careful.

Jane was quiet until they pulled out of the parking lot, but before they started discussing their approach, she had to rib her friend just a little.

"That was a nice, tender moment back there. What did the handsome Commander have to say?" Kate accepted it for the teasing it was meant to be and told Jane that he told her to be careful, be smart, watch out for each other, and that he'd see them as soon as the warrant came through.

Kate was behind the wheel for this trip, so without ever taking her eyes off the road, got serious with the trainee on her expectations.

"You will stick close to me, and you will follow my orders. I hope you remember the silent hand signals you learned at Quantico, because we're more than likely going to use them."

Jane's nerve endings felt prickly, almost like her body had been zapped with an electrical charge. The adrenaline boost felt so strong that she had to tap her toe to calm the sensation. In spite of how her body was reacting, Jane felt energized in a way she'd never felt before.

Kate glanced her way, and continued, "It's normal to be a little nervous before a takedown, especially your first one, but stay calm and remember your training. Trust me and trust the team. We'll make the calls, just be damn sure you follow without question because we all want to walk out of these woods, hopefully with the bad guy in handcuffs."

Jane nodded her understanding as they pulled the truck over on the shoulder of the road where they had parked the first day. At the back of the truck, they wordlessly put on their Kevlar vests. The bold FBI acronym emblazoned in glow in the dark highlighter yellow, made them easy to identify. The gravity of what she was about to participate in became absolute as she mimicked Kate and unsnapped the retention strap on her holster to allow for easier access to her gun, but then quickly relaxed when Kate leaned against the tailgate and removed her Chanel Slingbacks. The distraction Jane provided when she commended Kate's decision to change into shoes that were more appropriate for the woods, or chasing down suspects, added just enough levity to ease the tension without detracting from the laser focus they needed for their mission.

Looking at the image of the plat map on her phone, Jane told Kate, "The private parcel is up the hill and east of here, and by the looks of it on the map, it isn't too far." Kate nodded and then headed up the hill with Jane right behind her. At the top of the hill, Jane checked the map again, and then opened her phone's compass app and pivoted to her right.

"The property line is about 1000 yards in this direction," she said, and noted that it was in the opposite direction of the path they'd walked to Allison's final resting spot just four days earlier.

The agents' footfalls overturned the blazing red and orange leaves that had blanketed the ground, and while the hardwood trees were bare, their towering limbs still cast an apron over the mid-day sun. As Kate started to tell her partner that they'd need to stop short of the presumed property line because they had no legal right to enter it, her phone buzzed in her pocket.

"That was Bill," she said, "we have our warrant, and they're on their way. They're coming in from the road though."

Jane nodded at Kate and waited for her next command. The walk from the car helped her calm the restless energy that had trundled through her, so she replayed the instructions she'd been given because she planned to follow them without question. She trusted Kate and the team with her life, and wanted more than anything to prove to them that they could trust their lives to her, as well. Jane hoped it wasn't too late to do that, because as much as her nerves sparked through every stitch of her body, she was confident she'd be able to fulfill her role and contribute to the operation.

Kate broke from her quiet thoughts, and told Jane, "Bill told us to wait for them to arrive, that we shouldn't approach without backup."

"Okay," Jane responded. "I guess that makes sense. Will he let you know when they're close?"

Kate smirked at Jane, and said, "You didn't let me finish, rookie." Turning serious again, she added, "I'm not sure Kacey or Vanessa have time for us to wait."

Kate's pensive moment after reading the text now made sense to Jane, so she spoke the words she felt sure her friend was thinking. "Are you thinking we should go in, now?"

Kate looked on and started to answer, but Jane interrupted, and with a smirk said, "You didn't let me finish, boss. I agree with you that our delay could mean the difference between life and death to those two ladies, but will also add that my career is already in jeopardy, yours is not. Are you sure you want to do this?"

"Bill and the reinforcements are probably only about ten minutes behind us when you figure in that they're driving, and we're hiking." Kate looked up at Jane, and continued, "My plan is to approach and observe-for now. I will make the call on if we go in once I can assess the situation in real time. I do not want two more dead victims if we can help it, but I don't want to be reckless, either. What do you think; you up for it?"

"I'm in," Jane declared, and in another attempt to distract from the dire urgency, continued, "As much as I like and respect Maura, I really don't want to go back to her place of business." Jane seemed to understand that Kate's hesitation had less to do with herself, than it did with her.

"Don't worry about me, I'm ready for this. As you said, I've been very well trained, but more than that I trust your judgment completely and will follow your lead unquestioningly. I know you have my back, and I will have yours. You can count on me, Kate."

Kate nodded, and together the two agents checked the plat map and got their bearings. With her index finger held up to her lips, Jane recognized Kate's signal that it would be silent communication only. Even the slightest noise would reverberate and echo through the naked trees in the woods. Mimicking Kate's soft and steady footsteps, Jane was careful to leave enough space between them so if given the signal to halt, she'd be able to do so without colliding into her leader's backside. Both of their heads were on a silent swivel, looking for threats as they crept along their planned route.

Startled by the deep-toned honking of geese as they settled into their migrating V formation, Kate stopped their advance and pointed to the sky beyond them. Jane noticed the plumes of smoke wafting skyward and shared a look of acknowledgment with Kate that she too was aware they were headed toward a dwelling of some type. They resumed their silent advancement knowing that the smoke was a clear indication that someone had either recently been inside the structure, or was still there.

Kate's fisted left hand shot up quickly and Jane halted, then stepped up beside her when Kate motioned with her hand to do so. From their vantage point behind the trunk of a tree, the ladies saw a white van parked between two buildings and an open barn door, but no other movement. Jane rested her right hand on the butt of her gun, and awaited instruction from Kate who did the same, and then pointed to another tree wide enough to conceal them, but closer to their target. Jane understood her role was to watch for anything that might threaten Kate's safe passage to cover. Once she was concealed, Kate would provide the same cover for Jane.

Their closer vantage point put them in a better position to hear any type of movement, which would help Kate make the decision whether to move forward. Suddenly the forested woods, and all the creatures that inhabited it seemed to go silent, as if they were aware of the vital pursuit the agents were undertaking. In that almost surreal quieting both Jane and Kate's attention was drawn toward the barn.

"Did that sound like a groan?" Jane whispered.

Kate's affirmative nod prompted both agents to unholster their guns, and start a speedier yet still silent approach toward the open barn door. Jane's whole body seemed to buzz with the hope and anticipation of rescuing the New Mother Killer's newest victim, and while the progression toward the groaning noises seemed interminable, she recognized that a hasty approach could be deadly, and followed Kate's path without question. She was thankful for the size of the trees because the concealment allowed them to scan for threats between themselves and the wide-open area of the door where they'd be most vulnerable to an ambush.

CHAPTER 42

DAY FOUR - 1:00 PM

Rural Land – Oakland County

The wail of sirens in the distance interrupted their quiet surveillance, and with one more swivel of her head, Kate gave Jane the nod that it was time to cast off. Kate stepped out into the open and with a two-handed grip brought her gun from its at-ease position at the side of her leg.

Jane did the same, and with their weapons out ahead of them, they leapt the final distance to the open door without incident.

"FBI!" Kate bellowed as she crossed the threshold, but she was met with only the muffled groans of the incapacitated occupants. Jane knew from her training that protocol demanded the scene be cleared of any hidden threats before all else, so despite her instinct to rush to the aid of the victims, she went right to Kate's left. With her weapon leading the way, she began the first real time sweep of her career.

"Clear," she shouted, which was answered by Kate with the same assurances from the left side of the barn. Jane holstered her gun and sprinted toward the bleeding victim in closest proximity to her while Kate raced toward the hogtied woman with her phone at her ear. She heard Kate telling Bill that they needed rescue squads STAT and would need crime scene in here as well.

Jane knelt beside the man she recognized as Luke Johnson, and was assailed by a visual image of puzzle pieces falling into place. There's time for that later, she thought, and re-centered her focus on the man clutching his stomach on the concrete before her. Jane studied the bloody pool beneath him and noticed a stain that had grown to the size of hula-hoop was already turning reddish-brown, which indicated it was starting to dry. Luke's hands were pressed against his stomach, and when Jane saw that the fresh blood flow had slowed to just a trickle, she knew that the emergency medical team would be too late to help him.

"Is that Kacey?" she yelled out to Kate, but before she could reply, Luke struggled to lift his arm, and squeaked weakly, "That you, Janey?" His raspy words jolted her back on her heels when he added, "Your daddy is not happy with you."

As if he'd paid a final homage to his own higher power, Luke Johnson turned his head to the left, and through his open mouth sputtered the last ounce of blood his heart would ever pump.

Jane placed his hand gently back on his stomach, then stood up and ran to Kate who was trying to remove the saturated gag from Kacey's mouth. Jane snapped on her nitrile gloves when she realized that Kate wore hers, then took a minute to look around at their surroundings. There was a stone fireplace toward the back of the building, and when she noticed a metal rod and spool of yellow nylon rope leaning against it, and partially charred plastic in front of it, Jane felt almost clammy and weak kneed.

The sirens coming closer broke her out of her reverie, and as she bent down to help her partner with the panicking woman, she whispered to Kate, "The man was Luke Johnson. Took a gut shot. Bled out and died as I arrived."

Kate nodded at Jane as they both considered the best way to help the terror-stricken woman. Her hog-tie restraints kept her on her side, and with the violent way she was shaking her head, getting to the dirty rag was a challenge.

"Kacey," Kate said calmly. "Do you hear the sirens? You're going to be okay. We're with the FBI, and are going to get you out of here, but I need you to settle a little so I can get your mouth free."

Jane noticed what looked like tiny hedge clippers on the cement beside the captive and handed them to Kate, who carefully snipped the cloth behind her ear where there was some slack and set it aside. Kacey's body shuddered as she forced her starved lungs to draw air. She turned her head toward her rescuers, and with trembling lips pleaded with them to cut her free.

Kate sat down on the filthy concrete so she could look Kacey in the eye and told her, "The medics will be here to cut you free in just a minute. We don't want to do more damage, so just try to hang on and stay still. Do you think you can do that? I'll be right here, and will not leave you, I promise."

Once Kacey calmed down, Jane directed her attention outside, and then nudged Kate with the toe of her boot and pointed at the white van that seemed to be rocking. Second guessing her decision not to take the time to clear the van, or the house, Kate nervously asked Kacey if she knew where the man who'd abducted her was.

It was clear that her mouth and throat had been completely depleted of moisture when, in a gravelly voice, she uttered, "They shot that guy and then left on a gator."

"They?" Kate questioned. "There's more than one?"

On Kate's nod, Jane unholstered her gun and ran outside. She didn't expect Tally or a partner to be lying in wait, but however remote the possibility of an ambush was, she was trained to be ready. She stepped onto the running board as gently as her size nine boots would allow, and peered in through the driver's side window. Both front seats were empty, but over the din of the blaring sirens, she felt certain she heard a faint whimper, and jumped off the running board and ran to the back doors.

With her gun aimed at the doors, Jane banged on them with her fist, and bellowed, "FBI! Come out with your hands empty and so

I can see them. NOW." But instead of the shuffling noises she'd expect if the occupants were taking up position, the faint whimper became more of a strangled cry. She pushed the door handle down to unlatch it and took two steps backward, because it allowed her to use the door as cover. Jane knew that if she had walked into a baited trap, her adversaries would either jump straight out, or start shooting, and she'd be ready for either one.

When all she heard was a muted plea for help, Jane cautiously stepped out from behind the door, and holstered her weapon. Although the blackness of her pupils concealed the deep brown of her eyes, Jane knew that the terrified woman in the van was Vanessa Anderson, whose life was undoubtedly spared by Tally's need to flee in a hurry. She didn't spend time questioning the details of it all, or the possibility of a partner and where they could have gone on a gator, and focused solely on the victim. Jane shouted for Bill and got into the van with Vanessa.

Gaining her balance from the rocking when she jumped in and squatted down, Jane noticed at once that while Vanessa's hands and feet were restrained, they hadn't been roped together yet, so she helped her to a sitting position.

"My name is Jane, and I'm with the FBI, we're going to get you home. Your husband, and Murray are waiting." Jane was grateful that the knot in Vanessa's gag hadn't been there long enough to tighten up too badly, and as she was untying it Bill stopped at the back of the van.

"Hi Vanessa, we're awfully glad to see you," he told her. "The paramedics are here and they're going to cut those zip ties off." Between quiet sobs and deep breaths she nodded thanks to him.

When the EMT's rolled up with their stretchers, Jane jumped out of the van to give them room to work.

"Have you been in the barn yet?" she asked her boss. "Are the paramedics working on Kacey? She's in pretty bad shape."

Bill nodded and told Jane that Kacey was already enroute to the hospital, and that the husbands had been called, and were going to meet them at St. Joe's in Pontiac.

Leading Jane away from the van and toward Kate and the rest of the crew, he told her, "Dr. Maura is on her way. Crime scene is processing the barn and the deputies are searching the house, and we need to find that gator."

Grateful for the update Jane nodded, "Kacey indicated there were two men," she said, "Have you been able to confirm that yet?"

"We're all meeting under that tree for a quick brief," Bill answered. Jane wasn't sure if he had to pick up his pace to keep up with her long stride, or if he felt the same sense of urgency she did, but their speed walking had become almost a jog by the time they reached the gathered task force.

They both accepted water bottles from Sam, and greedily drank before Bill got started.

"I'm going to be brief for now because we need to establish the most probable escape route, and we don't have a lot of time. First of all: Sam, was your deputy able to locate Sanchez?"

"No, sir, he wasn't. The front desk manager is a hunting pal of his, so he let him into Sanchez's room. It had been cleared out. He did mention, though, that as he was pulling in the parking lot he noticed a white van pulling away from the curb."

"Okay, that rings true with what Kacey told us about there being two of them, so we have to assume that Sanchez is the second man. How deeply he's involved is to be determined, but we must approach them both as hostile, with nothing to lose."

Jane took another gulp from her water bottle and tried to quiet the racket in her brain so she could process and box up the thrust of puzzle pieces she was overloaded with. They still had a murderer to catch, so obsessing about Luke Johnson's connection to her father, or that the gooseflesh Sanchez caused with his icy stare was not imagined, was not a luxury she could afford in that moment. Jane tuned back into the briefing comforted by the fact that once the madman, or men, were in custody, all the connections would be made, and the puzzle would be complete.

It was Seth who reminded them that they'd already determined their killer would have access to a gator or a 4X4 of some sort in order to transport them.

Kate continued, "His profile tells us that in his mind, he's found his true calling, which leads me to believe that those first two kills were special to him, as were the disposal sites. We also know that Eve did not technically die by his hand, so she was just discarded like trash on the side of the road."

"I agree with Kate," Seth said, so if we're following his profile, we'd have to assume that he headed back to that acreage of state land. You didn't by chance hear the revving of engines, or notice any disturbances in the woods when you were hiking in, did you?"

Jane fielded that question and told them that they went in the opposite direction of where Allison and Mandy were found, and that they didn't hear a thing.

"And we were hyper vigilant, so I'm sure we'd have picked up on anything that didn't blend in with the natural surroundings."

Kate nodded her agreement, and Jane continued, "Keeping in mind that the acreage was the original Mother Killer's safe place for 15 years, and that his former cellmate was found dead in Tally's den of evil, it can't be ignored that they were working together. So, it would make sense that in Tally's twisted mind, he'd find refuge by getting as close to his demigod as possible."

With all four of the agents in agreement with the assessment of where he'd go if he were on the run, Seth told them he was going to put Abbey on a facetime call.

"Maybe she can find something that'll help us map our way in."

"Hello to all my dears. Your success in finding Kacey and Vanessa is all the buzz around here," Abbey said in her song-like tone.

"Hi Abs, and thanks, but we need some help, like 20 minutes ago fast."

"Watch my fingers fly at the speed of light. What do you need?"

"Any information on the state land that abuts Tally's where the first two women were dumped. We think they took off on a gator and headed that way, so anything you can tell us about access points from here would be great."

The entire team gathered around Seth, and on the small screen of his phone watched their analyst roll her chair from one computer monitor to the next.

The faint tapping of fingernails on a keyboard stopped as Abbey exclaimed, "Ah ha! I knew it. When I scanned the satellite photos of where you're standing, I also scanned the land you're asking about. You can thank me with a double caramel latte when you get back, but that land has a structure still standing on it and because I'm an analyst extraordinaire, I took a screen shot, and I have the exact coordinates. How was that for fast?"

"Abs, that is amazing," Seth said. "It is more than likely where Tally headed. If you can find a way in from here, I will provide you with your lattes for a week."

"Oh, you sweet, Italian grey fox, for that kind of a reward you'd need to challenge me a bit more. I've sent the coordinates to all of you, but due west from where you're standing, there appears to be a narrow opening that you could probably get your Expedition through. It doesn't go all the way through, so you'll have to hike the last bit in, but if you continue to head due west, you'll get to it."

"Thanks Abs, keep the line open for now, okay?"

The group all checked their phones for the coordinates, and Patrick spoke up. "There is no way a regular vehicle is getting through there, they sit too low, so Sam and I will take our men and access it from the road."

Bill agreed with the Commander and ordered that he and his three agents would traverse cross country, and meet them there.

"I need to caution all of you though," Seth told them, "Lloyd Tally is more likely to go down shooting, rather than surrender, and remember that he has nothing to lose, so suicide by cop might be his way out." It was understood among law enforcement that a lot of perpetrators will aim and even fire at them in order to draw gunfire to himself.

Bill quickly shook hands with the officers as they jumped in their vehicles, and then with his hand above his head, pointed to his truck and said, "You three, with me. We'll discuss our strategy in the truck. Hey Abbey, do you have us on your locator?"

"Yes sir, I do. I make it my business to always know where my angels are."

Bill smiled, and then told her they would keep Seth's phone connected, so if they veered off track she could correct them. Jane felt supercharged as she hopped into the truck because she'd worked toward and looked forward to this day for 13 years. She wasn't sure if it was her finely honed instincts or just a gut feeling, but she knew that by day's end, the first monster of her career would be in a cage. Where her career would take her, she wasn't sure, but her path forward would not falter away from finding justice. Finding victims alive and knowing that the capture of the person responsible was imminent gave Jane a buzz like she'd never felt, and one she was determined to feel again.

CHAPTER 43

DAY FOUR - 1:00 PM

Rural State Land

Tally held tight to the steering wheel of his John Deere gator, and was glad he'd chosen the utility vehicle with a roll bar, because the side-to-side jarring could easily cause a rollover. His route, while very well concealed, was through the middle of forested land, and not on trails groomed for recreational off-roading. He fondly remembered his mentor telling him about the lone structure, a forgotten gem hidden amongst the giant hardwoods that would provide temporary refuge if the need to flee in a hurry ever arose.

He smiled at the memory of his training and looked over at Sanchez who had his duffel bag clenched so tightly to his stomach that his fists were white, as if he'd cut off the blood flow to them. His eyes were like a doll's, wide open and fixed straight ahead, and his body was so rigid and still that the word catatonic is what came to Tally's mind.

When the reverberating rumble of the side-by-side was pierced by the distant blare of sirens, both men jerked their heads to the side, and then looked behind them as if they feared they were being pursued.

Once his heart rhythm went back to normal, Tally told Sanchez, "Well, they found my lair quicker than I expected, but don't worry, they won't find us where we're going."

"Where are we going?" Sanchez huffed ."My team is smarter

than you think. They'll have us landlocked in no time. And just how far do you think we'll get on a four-wheeler?"

Tally's abrupt laughter had a brittle edge to it when he replied, "You mean your *former* team. You went AWOL, remember? And let me point out, *partner,* we're running because after your hasty retreat, our connection led to my den being discovered, especially since all Janey had to do was connect the dots.

"That's bullshit, Tally, and you know it. And how do you know she was even suspicious of me, much less share it with the group?"

Tally shook his head in disbelief, and then explained how everything he'd done to facilitate Jane's ruin had been orchestrated by her incarcerated father, through him.

"He even fed me information so I could begin perpetuating your hatred for her months before she even graduated from the academy. Do you think ole Abe came to rub your nose in her success on his own? Hell no, he didn't. Did you really believe you ever stood a chance to be chosen for that team? Hell no, you didn't. And do you think it's a coincidence that my killings started right after she was selected, and you were brought up to work the case with her? Hell no, it wasn't. It was a carefully executed ambush, planned for the sole purpose of ruining Jane's career in the FBI. To Tad, this was never about carrying on his legacy of murdering women."

Tally knew by Sanchez's unblinking stare that his words impacted him like a 95-mph fastball to the helmet, and since he still hoped for a partnership with him, he changed his tone and went on, "What he didn't plan on was me making the kills *my* priority, and changing his well-written script to develop my own style. But fear not, partner, we're almost at our hideaway, and we'll be safe there. I have a clean vehicle hidden under a camouflage tarp, and we're on public land so we'll be able to drive out of here like a couple of tourists."

Sanchez put his head in his hands, took a deep breath and asked for more details on how they were going to escape.

"Do you have alternate IDs, and a way to change your appearance?"

Tally tipped back his head and laughed, "With our mad skills on a computer, I'm sure we'll figure it out. Here's our temporary sanctuary, grab your bag and let's get started."

CHAPTER 44

DAY FOUR – 1:30 PM

Rural State Land

The path the agents were on was nothing more than a clearing between trees, Rather than risk getting the truck hung up, Bill kept it to barely above an idling speed. It seemed to Jane that she was not the only one feeling hyper alert with the buzz of bringing Tally's reign of terror to an end.

Seth broke the silence to discuss their plan of action. "The first thing to remember about a strategy, Jane, is that it must always be fluid and adaptable because often times the mission does not go exactly as planned." Jane was laser focused on his message when Kate chimed in.

"Field experience could mean the difference between life and death, and while you have great instincts, you do not yet have the experience. I'm not trying to freak you out, rookie, because you will be surrounded by over 30 years of field experience, and we'll have your back, but you *must* stay with us. You did great on our approach to Tally's barn, so again I'll say, remember your training, and follow our lead." Jane knew she would follow her team's lead because she trusted them and their experience and wanted nothing more than to learn from them.

"I can't stress it enough," Jane assured them, "I will not break with protocol and will follow your commands without question. I trust all of you. I also realize that your trust in me is mine to earn. I won't let you down."

All three of them seemed to understand that the meaning of her statement went beyond the task they were about to undertake, so Seth laid out his vision for how he saw it unfolding.

"We need to remember Tally's overwhelming need to feel seen in a world where he's always felt invisible, because playing to that ego may be the only way to diffuse a hostile situation. We also believe that his obsession with Wilkins began on the day of his arrest."

With his focus on maintaining control of the truck as it lurched side to side, Bill told them that he'd spoken with the unit-chief in charge of the Wilkins task force, who told him that Tally was not included in the apprehension team but went to the scene in his own vehicle.

"When they brought Wilkins out, he said Tally was outside watching and that it was almost creepy how he followed every slow step the killer took and didn't even blink until Tad was in the back of the squad car. That insubordination was another factor in his decision to exile him."

Jane had studied every gruesome fact of her father's case almost obsessively over the years, but it was the details she learned from the law enforcement side that drove her passion to be a part of it.

"We're going to have to stop in a minute and hike in," Seth said, "and I'd like to discuss having Jane, if the situation allows, step up and tell Tally that she remembers him from her father's arrest. It might start a dialogue, and the longer we keep him talking, the better the likelihood of a peaceful ending."

Jane listened to Kate debating the soundness of that idea, but in her mind, she was happy that the team seemed to look at her as an agent, and not the daughter of the man this case seemed to revolve around. The last thing she could have tolerated was if the group felt they had to dance around the topic in order to save her feelings.

Jane interrupted their back and forth on the dangers of putting an inexperienced agent face to face with a killer, when she raised her hand and announced, "I'd like to do it. Kate, I appreciate your concern, but I know I can handle this. By all appearances it looks like Tad was instrumental in these killings, and in trying to make me crazy. He, or someone in his realm, contacted my aunt, and that is not okay. If I don't do this, I'll feel like he's won. That monster took a lot away from me already, he can't have anymore. Please let me do this."

When Bill turned the engine off, Seth reminded them all to silence their phones, thanked Abbey for her spot-on directions, and then told her he was going to break their connection.

"Okay, good," she said, "but please, be as careful as you would be carrying a newborn baby across a minefield. I need my family to come home safely. Abbey Louise out."

At the back of the truck, the men strapped on their Kevlar, and Seth handed Jane and Kate an extra clip for their weapons. They still had their tactical vests on from their morning trek in. Bill took a long gun from the locked floor compartment, verified it was loaded and had one in the chamber, and nodded for the group to follow him. For the second time that day, Jane unsnapped the retention strap on her holster, and held the weapon down the side of her leg. As was decided on the ride, Jane fell into line in the third position behind Kate, and Seth took up the rear.

To minimize the risk of an ankle sprain or noisy entanglement with the branches or brush along their path, the agents maintained a slow, almost feline pace through the woods. The skyscraping trees, while stripped bare for the winter, still provided them with enough cover behind their massive trunks to take stock of their course as they advanced. As she had when she made the noiseless trip with Kate earlier, Jane felt energized and alert in a way she'd never felt before. It seemed like the tension that came with the anticipation of a possible showdown with the bad guys gave her a boost far more exhilarating than the caffeine she craved so much.

Deep, angry voices carried through the trees at the same time Bill held up his left fist. Jane recognized the signal to halt and drew up silently beside Kate. After a pause, Seth got the silent cue to join Bill in the lead position. Bill pointed at them, one by one, and motioned for them to advance and form a semi-circle in a small copse of pine trees, behind which stood a small log cabin. A metal roof covered in shriveled, brown pine needles, extended over a cement slab where two men were engaged in a heated conversation. Their arms pitched up and down like an orchestra conductor, and their nose to nose, bent posture made it clear they were arguing.

In a voice they recognized as Adrian Sanchez's, they heard, "All I wanted to do was tank her career. I never signed on for murder. I should be a blonde Irishman on my way to Fiji right now."

The second man whom they knew to be Lloyd Tally, snapped back, "Hey, you invited yourself to *my* party, and the party isn't over."

The agents all went on high alert with Tally's next assertion, "Do I need to remind you whose gun killed that sap in the barn? Just admit to your sanctimonious self that we're partners. Once I train you, as Tad trained me, we will be the best killing team of all time." After his tirade, he lowered his voice, so the team surveilling them had to struggle to hear him.

"Just admit it Adrian, you enjoyed watching the new girl squirm in the back of the van, and got off on how her saucer sized eyes seemed to plead for mercy. I'm offering you the opportunity to relive, and even top, that experience."

Jane remembered a class on the psychopathy of a serial killer, and how her professor, from the Behavioral Analysis Unit told them that most of the time the reason a serial killer has for murdering people makes sense only to themselves. He went on to stress that as agents they'd have to learn to be okay with that, and to just take the win when they bring him or her down. As meditative as Jane had become with that memory, her statuesque form, and laser focus never wavered, so when she saw Bill raise his hand in the air, she knew go time was imminent.

As he began counting down from five, one finger at a time, Jane engaged the deep breathing exercises she'd been taught as a way to slow her heart beats, exchanged a reassuring glance with Kate, and was ready to step out of concealment once Bill's hand became a closed fist.

Bill led with the rifle, while the other three held their Glocks with the standard, two-handed grip, and stepped into their suspects' line of vision.

"FBI!" Seth shouted. "Hands where we can see them and turn slowly toward us."

It was clear that the infiltration of what they thought was a safe haven startled the men into immediate compliance, and as they turned without a weapon toward them, Seth looked to Bill for a nod, and then motioned for Jane to move forward. Kate looked at her as well, and without moving her mouth, told Jane to stick with the script and that she had her covered.

Jane took a small step forward and holstered her gun before she proceeded closer. With her empty hands at her sides she stared directly at Tally because Sanchez's icy glare, while less nerve scattering than before, could still be a distraction.

Confident in her team's back up, Jane told Tally, "I remember you from the day my father was arrested." She watched for facial cues that he'd processed her words, and when she knew she had his undivided attention, she continued with the lie, "You watched him as closely as I did."

Jane realized that her next question was meant to engage Tally in a conversation but was ready in case the outcome went in the opposite direction.

"I also remember that your eyes were as locked on my father's as mine were. I know he saw me because he stared back with nothing but hatred. Did his eyes speak to you, too?"

Tally and Sanchez stood rock still and remained mute just long enough for Jane to relax and take a slow step backwards when, with magician quick hands, Tally removed a gun from the back of his waistband and wrapped his other forearm around Sanchez's throat. By the time he had the pistol aimed at his hostage's head, the rest of the team, guns still drawn, had advanced.

"You all need to step back and holster your weapons, or I will put a bullet through his head and start shooting."

Jane kept her weapon trained on Tally, but remained cued into the team, prepared to follow their lead if they did retreat. Kate motioned her back, while Seth stepped up closer to the armed man. With both his arms extended at his sides, he made it obvious he was holstering his Glock.

"You're a trained agent, Tally, and you know this isn't going to end well if you don't put down your weapon. Do you hear all the sirens? The only way out for you, is through us."

Despite the intensity of the wailing sirens, Tally's unblinking stare remained vacant, and he made no move toward surrender. Sanchez's eyes were opened wide and seemed frozen with fear, while the lower half of his body trembled with obvious distress. Jane's head remained fixed, but her eyes roamed side to side at her team, and her hands remained steady as they stood poised and ready to end the standoff.

Seth took another step and positioned himself directly in front of Tally.

"If you so much as twitch with your trigger finger, you will be dead before you ever get a shot off, and everything you've done in the last week will be reduced to one small newspaper article about a shootout that killed two disgraced FBI agents." That seemed to get his attention, so Seth continued, "you will die as unseen and unknown as you lived. But if you lay down your gun, and come in with us, your methods will be studied and talked about for years. The whole world will know who you are, and what you've done."

Jane was so transfixed on Seth's method of de-escalating the situation that she had to remind herself to take a breath. They all watched what appeared to be Tally having an internal conversation as he weighed his decision to either live to have his story told, or to die. Sanchez's body seemed to relax, and his eyes, no longer transfixed with terror, seemed more resigned to the fact that Lloyd Tally would not be the only one arrested today.

Tally broke the intense silence when he flashed his teeth with a curling snarl, and, still holding the gun to Sanchez's head, addressed Jane.

"This was all about him hurting you," he muttered, "but I took it to a whole new level with my kills and was better than he ever dreamt of being. I even got Sanchez to be my partner." It was clear to the team that he was comparing himself to Tad Wilkins. He turned to Seth and continued, "You promise me that the world will know that the New Mother Killer bested the original one?"

Seth nodded his agreement, and after a lingering, drawn-out silence, Tally thrust Sanchez to the concrete, but before his knees hit the ground with a thud, Seth's weapon was unholstered and trained on Tally. The rest of the team leapt forward and made it verbally clear it was his final warning to drop the weapon.

As the Sheriff and State Police vehicles came to a screeching halt, Tally's lips rolled up in a curved smile that revealed his canines. His brief hesitation had the group standing ready, but then like a flash, his arched brows became lost in the folds of his forehead when he threw Sanchez's gun to the ground and locked his fingers on the top of his head. His motion commanded a quick, immediate approach by the agents. Seth removed a set of zip-ties from his pocket, and abruptly pulled Tally's arms together behind his back and locked them together.

"No need to be so brutish about it," Tally whined.

"I fastened them nice and tight to give you a feel of how those women felt." Seth motioned for Sam and Patrick to come forward and retrieve their prisoner.

As the new Mother Killer was being led away, he stopped and with a wintery smile as cold as poison, taunted, "Hey Janey, I'll give your regards to daddy dearest."

Jane met his dull clouded eyes and replied with a snarl of her own, "Tell him I won."

The rustling of papers redirected their attention to the man still on his knees under the portico, hurriedly trying to stuff papers back into the bag that had popped open when he was flung to the concrete.

"He grabbed me from the hotel, thank God, you found us in time." Kate grabbed Sanchez by the elbow to stand him up, and then handed him the fake passport he missed in his haste to clean up his mess.

Kate's tone dripped with sarcasm when she said, "Well, luckily you had your alternate ID with you." Then she faced Jane and offered her a set of handcuffs. "Would you care to do the honors?"

Jane accepted the offered restraints and was gratified when for the first time since she stepped on the plane, she was able to look the man in the eye and not feel her tiny neck hairs raise, or a cool tingle down her spine.

Cuffing his hands together behind his back, Jane made the first of what she hoped would be many arrests. "Adrian Sanchez, you're under arrest for accessory to abduction and murder-for now."

Jane took his elbow and walked him to a waiting squad car. Before she released him to the sheriff, she turned him square to herself and advised him that between the burner phone in his pocket, and the 'start a new life' escape kit he had in his briefcase, it was only a matter of time before more charges were added.

"Oh, and let's not forget the forensic accounting of your ledgers, and the trail Abbey is following on the pilfering of your parents millions. You do remember just how good our Abs is, don't you?"

The disgraced former agent hung his head and allowed Sam to guide him into the back seat and belt him in, but before he shut the door Kate stepped up and said, "Sometimes irony just jumps up and bites us in the ass, doesn't it, Adrian? It looks like you'll be getting a new ID after all; it'll just be in the form of an inmate number instead of a blonde Irishman."

CHAPTER 45

DAY FOUR - 4:30 PM

Ionia State Penitentiary

I can't say I'm surprised that the warden moved me from a level 2 back to a level V, which is where I started out 13 years ago. At the lower end of the security spectrum, I was afforded the opportunity to have a job, or share time in the yard with other inmates, which was critical to building and running the vast network I'd spent years building, not only inside the prison walls, but outside of them as well. The single occupancy exercise modules and dayroom at level V limits my exposure to only one other person, a guard I have yet to get a read on. I'm not concerned, though, because I will be able to earn my way back to the lower security level, I'm certain of that. It will just take some careful consideration, and of course, masterful manipulation, which is one of my crowning points.

I knew it was a risk to use Luke Johnson because of our connection, but because of his blind devotion, and now his death, there will be no conclusive trail leading back. I am a bit miffed that I had to learn about it all on the 13-inch television in the dayroom, all by myself, instead of hearing the details from one of my trusted contacts. If it had been my contact who was briefing me, he would have known better than to refer to Lloyd Tally as the New Mother Killer, or to call Adrian Sanchez a partner. Both the moniker and the inclusion of a partner were preposterous because neither one of those wimps did anything to earn them the right to be compared to me. When I can get back to work, I will see to it that Candace, the ill-informed anchor who reported from just outside of my sanctuary never does another news report.

I was able to detach from Tally when I watched the clips that came in from the network's helicopter as it hovered over his workplace, and enjoyed being able to see the body bag being placed into the medical examiner's van. When the ladies he'd left alive were whisked away, I felt almost like I was a part of it. When you're as evolved as I am the actual death of your captive is secondary because it only takes a minute. What's most exhilarating is the anticipation of it and knowing the people who love them will crumble at their loss. I kind of surprised myself when I felt that same euphoria over the live victims, because they'll never feel safe again. That is the kind of power and control a man as evolved as I am gets off on, and it's what drives me to continue.

The live feed from the helicopter ended, and the news report shifted to what was once the heart and soul of my reign, to the place I used to call my own. It should've gone to my daughter, but she couldn't handle its rich history, so it belonged now to the State of Michigan. The main house where I'd done most of my killing had been demolished, but until today my sanctuary, tucked back in the woods, had been preserved. And when I caught the image of Janey holding Tally and Sanchez at gunpoint on my hallowed ground, it touched a nerve.

She had layers of law enforcement officers backing her up, but she and her team were the main players in the standoff. That snapshot might make some parents proud, or maybe even a bit concerned for her safety, but I was enraged by it. I was livid when I learned she was aiming for the FBI, so I had my best hired muscle on the outside threaten her boyfriend, and his family with harm if he didn't stop her from going to Quantico. When that failed, I decided to keep the threat alive and used his brains in the financial division of my organization.

I had other puppets in place to crack her mentally, and ruin her career.

Watching her execute a perfect Weaver stance with her gun, and the confident, albeit smug look on her face when she cuffed Sanchez, I had to admit that even my alternate plan to end her career had failed. Fortunately, I am a master puppeteer and never revealed the strings I used to control the show. Of the two people who could link me to a crime, one is dead, and the smarmy attorney, Sal Faraci is missing and will never be found. And *that's* what makes me the smartest man in operation. It also continues to provide me with the autonomy, and the freedom, to keep doing what I love.

CHAPTER 46

DAY FOUR - 6:00 PM

Oakland County International Airport

For the second time in four days, Jane sat shotgun and watched lights on an airport's towers blink like the beacons they were intended to be. She knew the incandescent flashing served as a guide for the pilots, as well as a symbol of caution for passing airborne objects, but to her they seemed like a roadmap to change. When she saw the guiding towers at the beginning of her trip, she felt like her future was as bright as the lights that were intense enough to gleam through the misty fog. Today though, she felt as if the guideposts to her future had dimmed, because while she was still confident in her ultimate destination, her pathway was in question.

She and Kate had only a brief conversation of the day because they knew the full account would take place on the plane with the entire team, but she cut through so much of it when she summarized, "Today the good guys won. Two women will go home to their loved ones, three other families will get the justice they deserve, and the small, friendly village of Holly will sleep soundly once again."

Those words reminded Jane of her personal mission statement. Catching the bad guys and getting justice for those they hurt was her silent mantra while she trained, and the rush of it finally coming to fruition, did not disappoint. It was a buzz she would chase for the rest of her life. In what organization she wasn't sure, she just knew that while she might be looking at a mountain ahead of her, the ones she had climbed to get where she was right now, were just as high.

Kate parked the Explorer on the tarmac and left the keys in the ignition.

"Someone from the Detroit Field Office will be by later to pick it up," she told Jane, and then asked, "Are you ready?"

Jane grabbed her duffel from the back seat, adjusted her messenger bag so it rested comfortably at her waist and told her friend that she was ready, because she was. She was relieved when Bill told her that he wanted to meet with her before they discussed the case because she would not be able to move forward until she knew exactly how far back her slippery slope put her. So much had unfolded in the ten hours since she'd come clean about her covert activities and she was grateful to have been able to see the case through, but it was time to learn the consequences of her actions.

"Before we get on the plane," Kate told her, "I want to tell you something. When I was new, I went around my training agent and visited a man we all thought was the husband of our latest victim. He had a ten-year-old daughter whose doleful eyes made me heartsick, so I returned the locket her mother was wearing." Jane's first thought was that she'd taken evidence, but Kate explained that it had already been processed.

"I thought it might give the poor kid some comfort," she went on, "and it did, but as it turned out, her father was our unsub. My team figured it out and arrived just in time, but I could've been killed, and worse, his daughter may have ended up as collateral damage."

"Wow, just, wow!" Jane said. "I did not know that. Why are you telling me this now?"

"Because my training agent, whom I admired and looked up to, was so angry that she refused to work with me again. It was five years before she even spoke to me, and I value our relationship too much to let that happen. Jane, I have no idea what is going to happen to your FBI career, but wherever you end up, I will be your biggest cheerleader."

Kate left her astounded trainee behind and stepped through the open door of the plane. Jane snapped out of her trance-like daze when she crossed the threshold and was greeted by the soul soothing bouquet of freshly dripped coffee. Bill made eye contact with her from his seat at the back of the aircraft, so she helped herself to a cup and proceeded toward him, and ultimately, her future.

Jane sat in the rear facing seat, directly in front of her unit chief who was finishing up an apparent text conversation. Her attempt at getting a read on his body language was fruitless, so she settled herself in and enjoyed the rush her first drink of coffee provided.

"I should fire you," Bill stated as he turned his phone, screen side down on the seat beside him. "Your actions put you, and others in danger."

The hard swallow of the hot coffee helped alleviate the sudden dryness in her throat, but she knew he wasn't finished, and remained quiet. The dressing down was expected, and deserved, so Jane gave him her undivided attention.

"I told you at the beginning that I would not have a rogue agent. My team is the best in the Bureau because we function as a group and trust one another explicitly. Jane, you are without a doubt a rising star, but you're not the only star on the team, and if you try to run your own investigation, or hold back information again, I will fire you on the spot."

Jane's mind was slow to process that her career ambitions with the FBI were still alive, but she continued to listen intently as Bill went on to explain that he'd spoken with the director, as well as with Seth and Kate.

"We all agreed that your actions in the field were levelheaded and composed, and that you presented yourself as an agent willing and able to follow orders, and one who is eager to learn. All that being said, the director holds the ultimate authority and can reverse the decisions already made. You will meet directly with him once you complete your written report. I'll need a copy of it, too, and just so you know, that report will become a part of your service record.

Jane understood the words left unsaid and offered a silent prayer for help because she never again wanted her service record called into question. She knew a response was in order, but somehow felt that the standard monologue on how she learned her lesson was too cliché and unsuitable.

"Sir, there is absolutely no good reason for my bad choices, so I'm not even going to give them lip service. What I will say is that I learned invaluable lessons by being allowed to see the case through. I learned how much harder this job is when you try to go solo, and that I was much stronger, and more effective, as a teammate. I didn't fully comprehend what an opportunity I had when you put me on this team until my impulsive decisions threatened that spot. But mostly, through it all, I was reminded of why I chose this field, and I was devastated to think I'd lost my chance with the Bureau." Jane didn't want to sound confrontational or cocky, so she held back that in some capacity, she would continue to work in law enforcement.

Jane exhaled what felt like the first breath she'd taken since she sat down when Bill pulled a slow, genuine smile and stood up. She matched his motion and accepted his outstretched hand.

"I'm not going to tell you that we should all forget about this and move on," he told her. "That would be dangerous." As he took the lead down the narrow aisle toward the team, he added, "What I will say is that we're going to start fresh and move forward from this point."

Jane and Bill joined their partners in the same set of seats they'd used on the flight over, and as Jane sat across from Kate, she noticed the laptop on the small table between them. The grin that spread across Kate's face, and knowing they would be hearing the sing-song voice of Abbey again, left Jane feeling lighter, and more unencumbered than she'd felt in days.

Bill started right in with the re-cap of the day's events and told them all that the crime scene unit found enough evidence in Lloyd Tally's barn of barbarity to put him away for the rest of his life, and that Sanchez was currently on suicide watch, but in the custody of federal agents.

"Abbey has a lot of oars in the water. I'll text her and let her know we're ready so she can fill us in, but our team's case is closed. Everyone did good work with very little to go on." Making eye contact with Jane, he concluded, "Our team is solid."

The laptop's ringing drew their attention as the grainy picture of their Zoom call came into focus. Jane was reminded it was Halloween season by the cat-eared headband Abbey sported, and by the bat pencil topper that replaced the fuzzy kittens from their last conversation.

"Hello, my lovelies," she practically sang. "You're coming home victorious again, with an extra bad guy added as a bonus. Good job."

"Thanks Abs," Seth said. "Have you had any luck with your searches?"

"Oh, my favorite grey fox, it's as if you don't even know me. I tunneled so deeply, that I was able to turn over gobs and gobs of information to our forensic accountants. Adrian Sanchez thought he was so smart but unraveling his ball of yarn was cat's play for me, and at the center of it was his entire pathway to how he stole millions from his parents. And I have to add that he never gave me the warm fuzzies I get from the rest of you."

Bill couldn't help but grin at Abbey's expressive summary, and he knew that she occasionally needed to be prodded along. Before he could speak, however, she went on: "I know, I'm rambling, but now my brilliant burrowing skills are looking for that lawyer, Sal Faraci, and what his connection to Tad Wilkins and Luke Johnson could be. Those tunnels, unfortunately, seem to all drop off like a cliff, or smack me headfirst into a wall. I do know that Faraci is in the wind and off the grid. I will keep digging, but Wilkins and Tally both used disposable email addresses, which are temporary domains that are thrown away each time, so tracking them are almost impossible."

Bill was about to thank Abbey and let her go, when she held up her pencil and said, "I was able to find enough to send it over to white collar and they've opened a RICO case on Faraci's firm. My sources tell me that one of the financial wizards over there offered a plethora of dirt on the firm in exchange for witness protection. That's all I have for now. Abbey Louise out." When Jane heard Abbey's use of the word financial wizard, her thoughts went to Nick, and she briefly wondered if he was the secret witness. Shut that thought off, she thought, you don't even know what firm he works for.

No one in the group seemed surprised that they couldn't find a useable connection to Tad Wilkins, even though all signs pointed that way. Bill did tell them that the prisoner had been moved out of general population and into an isolated wing, with a higher security level.

"He has no contact with anyone, anywhere," Bill assured them, "so his ability to manipulate from inside has been stripped away."

"For now, anyway," Seth added, "but he is being watched, and we will get notification of any changes to his status. If Tally is to be believed, that rat-bastard set everything in motion to hurt Jane, and if you come for one of us, you come for us all."

Jane's anxiety at the thought of her father setting in motion the murder of innocents just to torment her, was allayed with a soothing sense that as a part of this team she'd never have to face the villain alone.

Bill interrupted the brief silence and said, "one final thing and then I'll let you relax till we land. It was very troubling to the director, and to all of us, that two veteran agents had it in their mindset to go so far off the rails." Seth picked up where he left off and explained that measures were being taken to evaluate, and change the psychological evaluations they all took, and to possibly make them mandatory every five years to hopefully catch agents at risk before they snapped.

"I just got the text confirming a contract the bureau has entered into with a very well-renowned, highly respected psychologist to review our current protocol, and make recommendations." Bill looked to Jane when he added, "We've contracted with Judy Newell to provide the assessment."

IONIA STATE PENITENTIARY

SIX MONTHS LATER... APRIL 2011

People like me are not ruled by lust, nor do we need instant gratification. People like me who are patient, and plan, are without question, the most successful at whatever path they choose. I just happen to choose what I now refer to as a controller of lesser minds, and if that control leads to torture or murder, all the better. People like me do not fit into the typical stranger-danger tag, nor are we like the dirty old men that parents try to shield their children from. People like me are experts at fitting in, and becoming what others want to see.

When the guard came for me today and told me that due to overcrowding, I was being moved back to a Level 2 general population cell, I was not surprised. I knew it was only a matter of time, and I also knew they weren't moving me because they rented my room to someone else. They were moving me for two reasons only, and my unequaled talent was responsible for both. First and foremost was the fact that because I'm so damn good at what I do, there were no lines connecting me to Tally's kills. Zero. Along that same vein, as a master of disguises, not only was I able to convince my guard that I wasn't anything like he'd been led to believe, but he also has the potential to become one of my disciples. Sometimes you just have to go along to get along, and to remember the simple formula, patience plus planning equal success.

People like me cannot change how they think, and they can't be rehabilitated, and people like me, desire neither.

~ THE END ~

Dear Reader,

Thank you for choosing my book.

If you enjoyed *Jane's Journey*, you're going to love the next book in *The Mother Killer Series*, where Tad will once again wreak havoc from the sidelines. It's going to be another thrilling ride as Jane and the gang hunt another sadistic serial killer. Follow me on Facebook at Jill Wagner-Author for updates and sneak previews on the next installment.

Also, before you leave I would really appreciate it if you would leave a review on Amazon and perhaps recommend *Jane's Journey* to other readers. Word of mouth, and Amazon reviews go a long way in helping other readers discover my books.

Thanks again,

Jill

Made in the USA
Middletown, DE
12 April 2023